Beam X111

by

Paul Fronda

Beam X111

First published in the United Kingdom in 2015
by Paul Fronda

Scripture quotations taken from the Holy Bible, New International Version.
Copyright©1973,1978,1984 by International Bible Society.
Used by permission.

Cover design by Martin Smith

Edited by Sheila Fronda

Proofread by Sheila Fronda

Forward

The writings of Father Joel.

The 13th Day of May in the year of our Lord 1513: Squire A'aeth's men called, inquiring about a silver cross, found on the body of Samuel Wright. It causes me great concern that the cross, which I nailed to a beam in the Derwin cottage, has been removed, as well as great discomfit and perplexity as to how the cross came to be in the hands of Samuel Wright. A heavy burden lies within my soul that the evil spirit in the room is not at rest. But, by the grace of God, the door to the room has been boarded, which is now the only containment of the evil spirit that lies within. God help anyone living in such a place if the boarding were to be removed, for who could stand such evil that would be unleashed upon them?

"I tell ye, Samuel, it's cursed. God help the people who live here!"

From the snares of the Devil,
Deliver us, O Lord.

PART 1

1

Samuel Wright, the builder, and his twelve-year-old apprentice, Harry, made their way down the steep hill to the waterfront salvage yard with a wagon pulled by two shires. The vapour from the horses' nostrils steamed in the frosty air as they held the weight of the wagon from running away down the hill.

"Steady!" Samuel said, as he pulled back on the reins and ventured through the gates.

"Look after the horses, lad. I won't be long," Samuel said, as he walked over to the shack where Pike was sitting.

"Good morrow to thee, Pike. It be a cold one today!"

"Aye that it be," Pike replied.

Pike, who had worked his way up from a boy, was now in charge of several men who were employed to drag ashore the timber remains of any ships that had been dashed on the rocks or sunk in battle. Rocking to and fro in his chair and puffing at his pipe, Pike looked up, to reveal a face weathered by the wind and salt spray over the years.

"What can I do for thee today, Samuel?"

"I've two cottages to build on Squire A'aeth's estate up on the downs, and I need some sturdy beams."

"Aye, ye be in luck! The storm last night washed up quite a few timbers. I've just finished collecting most of the beams. I reckon they've come from the two ships that went down out there. Rumour has it, t'was the King's ship, The Regent, and the French Cordellere."

"I heard the King's ship had been sunk. Who would have thought that the French could sink her, with all the Regent's guns? Was there many lost?"

"T'was not the guns, Samuel, that sunk her. Word has it the Regent came alongside and they boarded the Cordellere. I reckon those Frenchs couldn't admit defeat, and someone below set light to the powder magazine. A mighty explosion took both ships down. I wouldn't 'ave thought there were many survivors - they went down pretty quick. They say that most of the crew on both sides perished. The Regent alone 'ad two hundred sailors, one hundred and eighty-five soldiers and thirty gunners, but I reckon there was more though."

"A wicked waste of life! God help them."

"Amen there, Samuel," replied Pike.

He knocked out his pipe, rose from his chair and took Samuel over to show him the pile of beams.

"There are some big main deck beams here in tact, and smaller ones over there."

"What's that pile?" asked Samuel, pointing.

"They're for burning."

"What be wrong with 'em?"

"Apart from being charred by fire, gun shattered, with bits of flesh, hair and blood on 'em – nothing. Would ye be 'aving a use for them?"

"By the looks, one or two bits. If they're going free, I'm not fussed about what state they're in. The lad will have 'em cleaned up in no time."

"I said nothing about them being free. Pay me a shilling and ye can 'ave them."

"But ye said ye were burning them."

"That were before I knew thee would be wanting them."

"They're not worth a shilling, they're all broken and burnt."

"If they was in good condition, I tell thee, they'd be worth four times that amount!" replied Pike. "And times are hard. Will ye be 'aving 'em or not?"

"Aye, ye be all heart, Pike," replied Samuel.

"Bring the wagon over, I'll get Will there to help thee load."

Will came over. He was a tower of a man with square shoulders and big, muscular arms that were developed from years of lifting heavy beams.

"It's these six . . . begins here," Samuel instructed.

Samuel started to bend down to lift one end of the beam but was stopped by Will saying, "I've got it." Samuel was astonished at Will's strength. He knew that an English oak deck beam could weigh up to three quarters of a ton, but with the ease that Will lifted the beam, it might as well have been made from some lightweight timber. Samuel marvelled as he lifted one end up onto the wagon and then the other, but he soon realized he was wasting time watching, and went and found the lad to put him to work, sorting through the broken beams.

"All done!" Will called out.

Samuel went back over to check the load. "If ye ever be needing a job, come and see me. I could do with someone with thy strength," he said.

"Thank thee kindly, sir. I'll bear that in mind," replied Will.

Samuel looked over to see how the lad was doing. He was just standing, looking down at the beams.

"What ails thee lad?" Samuel called out.

The boy didn't answer so Samuel walked over to see what he was staring at. Harry had uncovered a partially burnt beam that had a bloody handprint on it. But what held his attention was the shape of a sinister-looking face in the grain.

"That's nothing, lad - it'll soon scrub off. We can't be fussy. Timber's scarce these days – what with the war and all the boat building. Put thy back to it and sort the rest."

"It's not the handprint, Mr Samuel. There's a face on that beam!"

"There's no face, lad. Ye must be seeing things that aren't there. Ye have too much of a vivid imagination! Now get on with it."

As Harry started to pick it up, the seawater in the beam made the blood run down over his arms to the floor. Samuel went off to the hut to pay Pike while the lad finished loading the small beams onto the wagon.

"I might be back, end of the week, if I need some more," said Samuel.

"By the sounds of them guns out there, I expect I'll be having some more by then. Hopefully they'll not be English timbers!"

"Aye, to that!" replied Samuel.

With the wagon loaded, it creaked under the strain of the massive beams but the shires took it in their stride as they made their way slowly along the upward track.

Samuel, being a master builder and a good teacher, wanted to know how much the lad knew. He asked him what he thought the red on the beam was, and how a handprint got there.

"I'm not sure, Mr Samuel," said Harry, "I've never seen the likes of it before."

"It's blood lad!"

The boy's face went white as he looked down at the red stains on his clothes and tried to wipe them off.

Laughing, Samuel said, "Ye need to get used to a bit of blood, lad! There's plenty of it being shed nowadays."

"How did it get there? Whose blood is it?" asked Harry. He didn't dare say anything more about the face.

"Whoa! Slow down with all the questions, lad. Probably from some poor soul being in the wrong place at the wrong time when one of them French guns went off."

"Did it blow his hand off?"

"A little more than his hand, I suspect, lad!"

"Have ye ever been to war on a ship, Mr Samuel?"

"Thank God, I haven't, lad, but as a boy I worked with my father on board doing repairs out at sea for months on end. That was bad enough."

"What were it like?" Harry asked.

"What were it like? I'll tell thee what it were like. We slept on deck - that's if ye could find a spot. God help thee when there was a severe storm! Fresh food and clean water were on hand at first. After a while the water became yellow and stinking, then ye drank beer instead. All we had to eat every day was ship's biscuits, and most of them reduced to a powder that was full of worms - often mixed with rat's urine. Salted and smoked meat or pickled food was all right when we started out but it soon went rank. If ye wanted fresh meat, ye caught the rats and mice that were on board."

"Ye've eaten rats and mice!"

"When there's no meat and ye be hungry lad, ye'll eat anything. Oh and there was no changes of clothes - ye wore them day and night, and, of course, we mustn't forget the diseases that were rampant: dysentery and scurvy."

"What is scurvy?" the lad asked.

"Scurvy - it rots the gums, which made ye spit putrid, black blood. Worse still was, the men's legs would turn black with the blood, and the only way to release it was to cut into the flesh with a knife each day. So ye ask, lad, what were it like? Them were *good* conditions. Now, take all that and add to it the fear them men had to put up with, as they heard them French guns, not knowing if it was *their* ship that was next to be torn through with steel canon balls."

Harry looked extremely concerned.

"Don't worry, lad. If ye work hard at the job ye won't end up on one of them ships." He knew the chances of being enlisted were high, but he didn't want to alarm the boy in case it affected his work.

"What sort of name is 'Pike'?" asked Harry.

"It's a nickname he got. He was in the King's army, in charge of the men who carried pikes."

"What's a pike?"

"It's a long spear about eighteen to twenty feet long, a fearsome weapon. The men that carry them can kill the enemy without them getting close. He served his time then came back to the job he had before the war. The man in charge of the yard didn't make it back, and so Pike was promoted to the job."

The light was fading as they arrived at the site.

"The sooner we get the wagon unloaded, the sooner we'll be going home, lad."

Using two long poles they levered the beams to the ground.

"We'll sort 'em out in the morning - that's thy first job. Now let's be going."

14

Samuel and Harry arrived on site at 6 o'clock in the morning.

"Break the ice off the water barrel, lad, and get those small beams cleaned up."

"Yes, Mr Samuel," he replied.

"Morning, Samuel. It's a brisk one this morning!"

"Aye that it be, Benjamin. Hot tea before we start?"

"Well thank thee kindly, Samuel! That'll warm the cockles of my soul."

By mid-morning, with the help of the hired hand, Benjamin, most of the upright timbers of the cottages were in place. Samuel's thoughts turned to Will at the salvage yard, whose strength would have made light work of the uprights and probably would have had them up in half the time.

Stopping for midday break, Samuel and Benjamin sat with their bread and cheese discussing the next step of the construction, while Harry continued to work on.

"Doesn't he stop?" asked Benjamin.

"When he's finished cleaning the beams. You finished them beams yet, lad?" Samuel called out.

Standing up with a smile on his face, Harry replied, "Yes, Sir, Mr Samuel. All done!"

"Even the one with blood on?"

"Aye, Mr Samuel, 'specially that one."

"Well, get thyself over here for something to eat. We got a busy afternoon ahead."

"What be the story with the blood?" asked Benjamin.

"The lad came across one of the beams that had a bit of blood on it. I told him a yarn, saying it was the blood of a crew member that had got blown up," chuckled Samuel.

Benjamin smiled.

As the sun started to go down, most of the horizontal beams were fixed in place on top of the uprights.

"We've done a fair day's work there, Benjamin! Same time tomorrow."

"Same time it is then. See thee in the morning," replied Benjamin.

"Get all those tools collected up, lad. I got a home to go to."

As they made their way home, Harry asked Samuel: "I noticed some of them beams have numbers marked on them. What do they mean?"

"They be identification numbers. The carpenter would carve it into the beam so as to help him remember where it must go while he's building the ship, or house. Well done, lad, for observing it."

Harry looked pleased with himself. After a few minutes' silence, Samuel asked: "What beam had a number on - for you to ask?"

"The one that had the handprint in blood."

"And what be the number ye seen on it?"

"It weren't very clear but I could make out four numbers: X111. Would that be a special beam, Mr Samuel?"

Samuel didn't say a word. He was pondering over how a timber with such a number on could have been used to build a ship, knowing how superstitious sailors were.

That evening round the meal table, Harry's mother asked how he was getting on, and what he had been learning.

"I'm enjoying it and learning so much, Mother."

"Thy father will be pleased with thee! Ye know how important it is for him that ye have a good skill. So tell me, what did ye learn today?"

"All about numbers," he replied.

"Numbers?" she asked.

"Aye. Do ye know why they mark the timber beams with numbers?"

"Nay. I haven't never noticed any numbers on beams," she said, looking up at the ceiling.

"Look! There's one - number seven marked at the end of the beam!" Harry said excitedly.

"Well, I'll be blowed! We've been here all these years, and that's been there all that time without us noticing."

"Did I tell thee about what I saw yesterday on the beams?"

"Ye might have but I don't remember. I obviously weren't paying attention. Tell me again."

"I were sorting out a pile of beams and I came across one with a **bloody handprint on it!** There were **bits of flesh** all around it stuck to the beam!" he said with relish.

"Weren't ye scared, Harry?"

"Nay, Mother, not I! Ye get used to things like that in my job."

"My, my, ye sure have grown up, Harry!"

His mother didn't ask him how it got there as she considered anything to do with death a bad omen.

"I've got lots more to tell - of whose handprint it was."

He was disappointed he couldn't tell her any more as she said, "If ye have finished eating, ye'd better get up to bed. Mr Samuel will be outside waiting at 5 o'clock."

Harry came downstairs to see his mother getting the midday food wrapped for him and his father to take to work. He greeted them both cheerfully.

"Morning, Son. Work hard today and make me proud," answered his father.

"That I will, Father. We are to start the upstairs of the cottages today."

"That sounds exciting, Harry," said his mother. "I pray ye will be safe up there."

17

"Mr Samuel won't let any harm come to me. He's always telling me things *not* to do."

"Well, make sure ye listen to him! Do ye hear, Harry?"

"Listen to thy mother, Harry. She knows what she's talking about."

"Aye, Pa."

"Now, if ye want to make an impression on Mr Samuel, ye had better get out and wait for him on the track. It always pays to be early," his mother said.

Harry gave his mother a hug and made his way outside.

"He's turned out a fine boy, but I do worry about him lifting them heavy beams."

"Ye worry too much, woman. As long has he keeps his head down and learns well he'll be alright in life, and anyway them there beams will build his muscles," replied her husband.

Having set his young apprentice to work, Samuel started to hoist up the upper floor timbers with Benjamin. Pausing after some time, Harry couldn't help looking at Mr Samuel and Benjamin walking fearlessly on the high beams. Because work on the cottages was making steady progress, Samuel announced, "We'll stop for a break when we complete this section." Then he called down to Harry, "Lad, do ye remember how I taught thee to put up a ladder?"

"Aye, Mr Samuel!"

"Well, bring that long ladder over here, and listen carefully to me. Rest it against the cross beam below me and steady the bottom."

"Is this alright, Mr Samuel?"

"Take the bottom out a little. It's too upright, lad."

"Like this, Mr Samuel?"

"It looks alright from here, but did ye steady the bottom?"

"I think so, Mr Samuel."

"Now go and find me a small beam about six feet long."

Harry ran off, to come back struggling with a beam. "Is this one alright Mr Samuel?"

"That will do, lad. Now, I want ye to try and pass it up to us."

Harry managed to lift it onto his shoulder. He had watched Mr Samuel do it many times, and wanted to impress him. Wobbling precariously, he made his way over to the ladder and started to climb. He could see the first cross beam in front of him, but knew he had the same amount of rungs to climb again to reach Mr Samuel. Soon his shoulder was feeling the weight of the beam as it pressed down onto his collarbone. He had forgotten to put the rolled-up piece of sacking on his shoulder to cushion the weight, as Mr Samuel had taught him. As he stopped for a brief rest and tried move the beam a little to relieve the pain, he could see blood dripping down his shirt. Thinking it was from his shoulder, he was horrified to see that it was coming out of the beam. But it was the face on the beam, grinning at him, and the gradual appearance of a bloody handprint that made him scream and lose his balance. As he fell backwards from the ladder the beam followed him down. His scream was stifled by a sickening thud as it fell on top of him.

Samuel and Benjamin feared the worst as they saw the lad lying there, not moving. Coming out of shock, they raced down and together they lifted the beam off him, but their fears were confirmed. The lad was dead.

"Is that what I think it is on his chest?" asked Benjamin.

"What?" replied Samuel.

"It's a bloody handprint - on his coat," Benjamin said.

"How on God's earth did that get there? gasped Samuel.

They carried Harry to the wagon and Samuel took him home to his parents.

Harry's mother heard the wagon pull up and looked out of the shutters. Samuel was alone on the wagon and her instincts told her something was wrong. It was only mid-afternoon and normally Harry wouldn't get home until seven. In the time it took her to open the door, Samuel was carrying Harry down the path in his arms.

"I'm so sorry - he fell."

She didn't say anything. She knew by looking at the injuries to his head that he was dead. Samuel laid him on the large pine table. "So sorry, so sorry," he said, leaving her weeping silently as she held Harry's hand.

The following morning Samuel went to work with a heavy heart.

"Shame about the lad. I suppose ye will have to find thyself another now?" said Benjamin, not realising how callous it sounded – in fact he was very disturbed by what had happened.

"I can't think about that right now," replied Samuel looking at him sternly.

"What do ye think made the lad scream like that? Ye would have thought he'd seen a ghost!"

Samuel didn't reply. His eyes were fixed on the beam, which still lay on the ground, surrounded by a dried pool of Harry's blood.

"What do ye see, Samuel?"

"The beam - it seems to have an evil imprint of a face on it, and the number X111 carved into it."

"I don't see any face nor number."

"There, man!" Samuel said, pointing, "The lad was right!"

Benjamin bent down to have a closer look. "By God! Where did that beam come from? There's evil in it, we have to burn it!"

"Nay! If we do, we won't be able to finish the wall section - it's the only one that's the size we need and a trip back to the yard would cost me two days."

"I tell thee, Samuel, no good can come of it - if ye use that beam in a house. It's cursed, I tell thee. Look at what 'appened to the lad. It was as if he was pushed off that ladder. I'm telling thee, it's cursed!"

"Nay, Benjamin, thy imagination's running wild. He just fell."

"Then how do ye account for that bloody hand on his chest? It weren't there afore he climbed the ladder. I tell thee, Samuel, it's cursed. God help the people who live here!"

2

"Whoa!" Jonathan Earwaker commanded the horses as he pulled on the reins outside their new home. He and his wife, Isabel, sat outside looking while the children jumped off the cart and ran to explore the place.

"T'is a fine looking home, Isabel! A lot bigger than the last one."

"Well, with this one on the way, we need it," she said patting her stomach. "Is that all ours?"

"I wouldn't have thought so," he replied.

"But there's only one front door. If it's two dwellings, how do ye get into the other?"

"Most likely from round the back. Mind you, t'is a strange set up. All I was told was it's the left one." Jonathan replied as he helped his wife down from the cart.

"Who's next door?"

"Not sure, Isabel, but by the quietness of it, I don't think they can have moved in yet."

"Henry, George! Come and help thy father unload!"

"What about the others, Ma?" Henry called out, reluctantly making his way up the path with George.

"They're too young and they'll be in the way," replied his mother.

Isabel left them to unload and went inside to see the rooms.

"What do ye think, Isabel?" Jonathan enquired as he carried in his prized chair and placed it by the inglenook fireplace. He was the only member of the family to have the luxury of a chair, which he had made himself. Everyone else had to make do with wooden stools.

"Aye, it's a fine place. I'm sure we will be happy here," she said, on her knees getting the fire started. When ye have finished unloading, I thought I might send Henry into the woods to try and catch us a rabbit. Perhaps, as a special treat, we could have rabbit stew for supper," Isabel replied.

"Sounds good, Isabel – if he can catch one."

"It's been a long day," Jonathan said, smoking his pipe and staring into the flickering flames of the fire. "What are ye working on there, Isabel?"

"I thought I'd start a family sampler with the date we moved in to hang on the wall," she said sitting opposite him.

"That will be nice, Isabel. Any problems with bedding the children?"

"Nay, I put the boys up in the attic room, and the girls in with us."

"Well, it's getting late. I've got an early start tomorrow up at the estate."

Isabel went ahead up the narrow, winding stairs as he made the fire safe.

Isabel had already kindled the fire, hung the kettle on the spit hook and started preparing the food before Jonathan came down.

"Morning, Isabel. Did ye sleep well?"

"Fine, Husband, and thee?"

"Had a few hours. Couldn't help thinking about the new job."

"It'll be fine. Just do what ye usually do."

"That's what I love about thee, Isabel, full of encouragement! What's it like out there?"

"Pretty cold. I had to break the ice off the well bucket," she said, giving him bread and cheese wrapped in muslin cloth to take with him.

Jonathan kissed her on the cheek and made his way outdoors while Isabel went back upstairs to wake the children. With her hand on the attic ladder she called up to the boys to get downstairs and start their chores. There followed a sound like thunder as the boys clattered down.

"Right, boys. Henry, organise thy brothers. There's the animals to feed, the goat to milk, eggs to gather, and wood to get in."

"Okay, Ma," Henry said as his brothers followed him out.

"Rose, after ye have taken care of thy baby sister, I'm going to show thee how to make pottage."

"Thanks, Ma. I've always wanted to try making it myself."

"Well, the sooner ye get done with thy sister, the sooner we can start. The rest of ye girls, I want this place cleaned from head to toe!"

Rose came downstairs carrying her baby sister, and put her in the crib. "All done, Ma," she said, eager to be taught how to make potage.

The water was already boiling in the pan over the fire. Under her mother's supervision, Rose chopped onions and cabbage and put them in the pan, followed by beans and some herbs.

"What's next, Ma?" Rose said eagerly.

"We need a little meat - it can be anything we have. Today it's dried bacon. Cut it up and put it in the pan, stir it and leave until it thickens, then it's ready."

"Can I tell Pa I made it, Ma?"

"Of course ye can, Rose! Now ye know how to make it, ye can do it every time we have it."

"Ma!" Henry called, rushing indoors. "There's a cart coming down the path with lots of people on it."

Isabel looked out of the small back window shutters. Her neighbours had arrived. "Rose!" she called, "Ann needs changing again!" and went outside to greet them.

"Welcome!" she said as she stood there with Henry. "I hope ye had a good journey."

"Thank thee, Ma'm," said the man as he climbed down from the cart. "Henry Derwin. This is my wife Catherine and our children."

"I'm Isabella Earwaker, but please call me Isabel. This is my eldest. He is named Henry too."

"T'is a fine name - fit for a king, Ma'm" Henry Derwin chuckled.

The lad stood there without saying anything.

"Henry!" said his mother.

"Good morning, Sir, Ma'm."

Seeing that they had a lot to unload, Isabel said, "I'll get Henry to help thee."

"But Ma, I still got all my chores to finish," he protested.

"Ye can finish them when ye have helped to unload."

"Thank thee, Isabel. That's very neighbourly of thee," said Henry Derwin.

Isabel hadn't had a good look next door, and had only peered in through the shutters. She was dying to compare it with her place, so she said, "I'm sure ye all

25

could do with a drink! I'll bring it round when ye have unloaded."

As Isabel came in with a jug of cider, Catherine greeted her with thanks.

"What's thy cottage like, Isabel?"

"It's nice, but comparing it with this, it's a little smaller from what I can see."

"I haven't been upstairs yet. Would ye like to see it with me?" Catherine said, cordially.

Isabel had been hoping Catherine would say that and replied, "Lead the way!"

The children were already up there running from room to room, exploring.

"Ma, can we have this room?" Tommy said.

"No, Ma. I saw it first!" his sister protested.

"Stop squabbling! Nobody is having this room. It's mine and father's."

Looking around the room, she noticed a little door at the side of the big chimneybreast. As she opened it, it revealed a large alcove.

"What do ye think, Isabel? I think four of the children will be all right in there."

"It's big enough to save them sleeping in thy bed!" Isabel said laughing.

"That's true. The eldest boys can have the upstairs room."

"That's what I did with mine. So how many have ye got, Catherine?"

"Ten - three girls and seven boys. And you?"

"Five boys and six girls and another boy on the way," Isabel said with both hands on her stomach.

"So twelve. How do ye know it's a boy?"

"It has to be, to even them up. And, anyway, I have a knowing what it is by the kicking."

26

"I know what ye mean.   Girls seem to be more contented. Twelve is a nice round number, Isabel," said Catherine as they made their way downstairs.

"Come round if ye need anything, Catherine."

"Likewise, Isabel."

3

Jonathan came in, looking tired but cheerful.

"How was thy first day, Husband?" Isabel asked as she put his meal on the table.

"Good. I think I'm going to like the job, Isabel."

"I said ye would."

"As usual ye were right," he said, making quick work of his meal. "That was a good potage, Isabel. I enjoyed that."

"Ye will have to tell that to Rose. It was her first time of making it. She was hoping ye would be home before I sent her upstairs."

"I would have, but I had a lot to do before I could leave. I'll tell her how good it was when I see her."

"I met the neighbours today," said Isabel.

"What are they like?"

"Nice. Henry and Catherine Derwin. I got on well with Catherine; I think she's about the same age as me, maybe a little younger."

"That's a comfort to me - knowing that there's a woman next door, what with the new one on the way. Any children?"

"Yes, ten - seven boys and three girls."

"Oh aye, it's good to have boys about the place, Isabel."

"Yes, Husband," she said smiling.

"Jonathan, Jonathan, are ye awake?"

"What is it, woman?" he said, churlish at being woken up abruptly.

"I can hear a child next door crying. It's been going on for some time. What do ye think is wrong?"

"Nothing, probably having bad dreams. Go to sleep, Wife; I've got an early start in the morning."

Jonathan was outside backing the horse into the cart for his journey to work, when he heard: "Good morrow, ye must be Jonathan. I'm Henry."

"Morrow to thee. I heard that ye moved in. I pray thee had a good night?"

"Apart from one of the children having a bad dream, aye, good."

"My wife could hear. She was a touch concerned, but that's women for you," he said chuckling.

"That's about right. Anyway, must get on. Don't want to be late on my first day!"

"What position?" Jonathan asked.

"I'm head gardener," he said, harnessing his horse ready for the wagon. "And thee?"

"Same place. Wheelwright. Keeps me busy," he said as he climbed up on the cart.

They headed off towards the estate for the busy day ahead of them, leaving their wives to deal with the chores to be done in and around the cottages.

29

"I hear that ye are a wheelwright?" Samuel Wright said to Jonathan as he pulled up in his cart.

"Aye, that I am."

"The name's Wright. Samuel Wright. I'm the builder here on the estate. I was wondering if ye could have a look at the wheel on my wagon – it's giving me some trouble when it's loaded."

"Jonathan Earwaker. I'll have a look for thee, after work."

"Much obliged to thee, Jonathan. Tell me the cost when ye are done."

"Call it a favour, Samuel."

"That's mighty kind of thee. Let me know if I can help thee in return."

"Pa's home, Ma!" Catherine's eldest boy said as he rushed out to meet his father.

"Untack him, lad, and turn him out in the field."

"Okay, Pa."

Henry went on in, to be greeted with a peck on the cheek by his wife.

"Good day?" she enquired as she served up his food.

"Aye, good – but hard. I didn't realise there was so much land on the estate! I got talking to our neighbour this morning. I didn't realise he worked there."

"What does he do?" asked Catherine.

"Wheelwright. I think he'll come in handy, considering all the problems I've had with the wagon," he said, hungrily tucking into his meal.

"All done, Pa," the lad said, coming through the door.

"Did ye tie the gate, lad?"

"Yes, Pa."

"Now get thee upstairs. Ye need to help thy Ma tomorrow."

"Night, Pa. Night, Ma."

Jonathan turned over in bed to find Isabel wasn't beside him. Trying to see in the dimly lit room, he could make out his wife standing with her ear to the wall. "What are ye doing, Isabel?"

"That child next door is crying again. It woke me up."

"Come back to bed, Isabel. There's nothing we can do."

"I'm going to speak to Catherine in the morning and find out what's causing it. It's not normal for a child to be like that night after night."

"Yes, dear. Now can we get some sleep?"

After several hours of being up, Isabel had a little precious time for herself and sat down at the table for a few minutes, then she remembered that she was hoping to speak to Catherine. She set off next door with her youngest in her arms. Opening the door she called out, "Catherine! It's me, Isabel. Can I come in?"

As she came downstairs, Catherine said, "Of course, Isabel! I'm glad ye came round - I could do with a break from cleaning. I'll make us a hot milk and honey drink."

Sitting at the table, Isabel asked her about the child crying at night.

"I didn't think ye could hear him. I'm sorry he's been keeping thee awake. He's been having bad dreams since we've been here."

"Which of them is it?" asked Isabel.

"It's little Tommy. I heard him crying the first night and went to him. He was tossing and turning with no covers on and murmuring about voices. The only way I could calm him was to cover him up and stroke his head. The following night I felt a hand on my arm and, when I opened my eyes, he was standing there sobbing. When I

31

whispered, "What's wrong?" he said there was a scary face in the room and voices that woke him up. I tried to put him back to bed but he sobbed even more and begged to sleep with us. He looked so scared Isabel, so I kept him in with me."

"Are the girls okay, and all the others?"

"Yes, they're fine. It's just Tommy. There's something he doesn't like in there."

"I take it he's sleeping in the small room next to the chimney? The one ye said would make an ideal place for them."

"Yes, three of the girls are in there with him. As I said they're fine. It's just him."

"I thought that must be where the crying was coming from. Our bedroom is the other side of the wall."

"Sorry, Isabel. I'll try and keep him quiet."

"Let's hope he sleeps tonight," replied Isabel.

"Oh yes, Isabel! I am worried that he will wake George up. He will be so cross if he does."

"Why don't ye have a little chat with him tomorrow, to see if ye can get him to tell thee more about the voices?"

Having finished her morning work, Catherine called Tommy in from outside where he was playing with the others. Sitting him on her lap, she said, "Tommy, I need to speak to thee about the scary face and voices. Tell Ma where the face is and what ye hear. Try and tell me word for word."

"The face keeps looking at me. It's scary, Ma! Then there's a big bang that wakes me up, Ma, like Pa's gun but louder and then voices. They keep saying, "It's so hot! We're burning! We're trapped! We've got to get out before it goes down!"

"It's just bad dreams, Tommy. Now go off and play."

"Isabel, have ye got time for a chat?" Catherine called through the door.

"Yes, of course. Give me a short while and I'll come round."

Isabel came in, to see Catherine at the table.

"Thanks for coming. I had a chat with Tommy this morning and learned a little more about why he's crying every night." She related to Isabel all that Tommy had told her. "I can't understand how a little child can come up with such a story! Strange thing though, Isabel, I'm sure when I go in there to make the beds I can smell burnt wood. I mentioned it to Henry but he said it's probably from the chimney letting smoke through the brickwork. He's knows best, I'm sure; I don't know anything about that sort of thing."

"Have ye heard anything thyself coming from within there?"

"No - only the crying, but as it's almost in the same room, you would think we would hear voices and especially an explosion, so it must be just bad dreams. I'll have a quiet word with the priest after the service tomorrow to see what he thinks."

"Good idea, Catherine we'll see thee there."

"Morning, Isabella. It's a fine day - as beautiful as my wife!" Jonathan said putting his arms round her from behind.

"What are ye after, ye old charmer! I take it by the mood ye are in ye slept well?" she said, trying to prepare the food before they all came down.

"Can't a man pay his lovely wife a compliment without expecting something? As it happens, I did sleep well. What about thee? Did the child next door keep thee awake again?"

"Nay. If he cried, I didn't hear him. I must have been too tired. I forgot to mention to thee last night, I had a chat with Catherine. Even though Henry thinks it's bad dreams the lad's having, she's gong to have a word with the priest today."

"I am in agreement with him but, for their peace of mind, it won't hurt."

"Children, get yourselves down here! The food's on the table. We'll *not* be late for church!" she shouted up the stairs. Jonathan finished his food and went out to harness the horse and wagon.

Dressed in their Sunday best, they made their way to the church to be met by the priest at the door, welcoming every one in as they arrived. After the service Isabel could see Henry and Catherine talking to him.

"I hope he can give them some words of comfort," Isabel said to her husband.

"Always worrying about other folk, that's what I love about thee, Isabel!" he said, taking her hand.

Back at the cottage, having got the chores done, they settled down in front of the fire while the older children played outside.

"I've finished it!" Isabel announced as she held up the sampler she'd been working on.

"That looks very fine. I think we'll hang it over the fireplace so everyone can see. Now ye have finished that, I've a tear in my coat that needs mending," he said chuckling.

"Why didn't ye say? I would have left the sampler and repaired it for thee."

"I've only just noticed how bad it is, sitting here."

"Take it off and I'll do it now."

34

"So, Henry, what do ye think of the priest's suggestion about paying a visit?"

"Not sure, Catherine. I still say it's because the lad's not used to sleeping in a different room. Anyway, I don't want word getting around that we have a problem here. Give it another week; see if he settles down by then."

"I hope so, Henry. It's not just Tommy, it's Isabel next door that's not getting any sleep."

"Is Jonathan not being kept awake?"

"Nay, he's like thee - doesn't hear a thing. Ye men are all the same, sleeping like logs and snoring!"

"I don't snore!"

"Of course ye don't, husband. I'd better start getting the children to bed. Three of them have fallen asleep already."

"I'll be up in a moment. I'll just finish my smoke."

In the alcove room, Catherine finished tucking the four children in. She had an uneasy feeling as she closed the door so she opened it again and looked around. The room looked no different to the rest of the house so, closing the door again, she went upstairs to check on the others.

"All settled down?" Henry asked as he got into bed.

"Yes. Although, I don't know what it is, but there's an uneasiness in that room tonight. I think I'll go and check the children again."

"They're alright. Ye will only disturb them."

"If I don't I won't be able to sleep, and that might keep *thee* awake."

"Ye had better go check them then," he said turning over and pulling the covers over his head.

Catherine could see the four lying fast asleep but little Tommy, who was against the outside wall, had been uncovered when the others had turned over. Covering him up, she crept upstairs to check on the rest. Seeing

35

that they were fine, she slipped back into bed, to the sound of her husband's snoring.

Catherine was woken by crying from the little room. She laid there for a while hoping it would stop, but her motherly intuition told her to check on him. She got out of bed and tiptoed quietly to Tommy. He was lying, uncovered, hard against the wall. As she knelt to pick him up and take him back to her bed, she discovered he was ice cold! She knew something was wrong. "Tommy," she said as she tried to wake him. "Tommy, Tommy!" But there was no response, as his little body lay limp in her arms. Her desperate shriek: "**Tommy, wake up!**" filled the house and woke everyone. Henry hurriedly lit a candle and rushed over to the alcove, to find Catherine sitting on the floor cradling Tommy and sobbing uncontrollably. Henry knelt down beside her, trying to understand what had happened.

"He's dead, Henry, he's dead."

"How can that be, Catherine? He was all right when he went to bed, wasn't he?"

She was too distraught to answer.

"Catherine, look! He has blood on his gown."

Catherine looked down and saw what looked like a bloody handprint on Tommy's nightgown.

"How could that have got there?" Henry gasped.

Finding the strength to answer, Catherine said, "I don't know. It wasn't there when I put him to bed."

Henry raised the candle to shine its light around the alcove. What he saw made him stand up to examine the timber beam on the wall above where Tommy had been laying. He could have sworn there was a face in the beam looking at him, but, as he blinked, all he could see was a crimson bloodstain. Stretching out his hand, he touched the stain with his finger. To his horror, it was *fresh* blood that his finger smeared, but what held him staring at the beam was a face that appeared to be ingrained in the wood and a carving of the number ℵ₁₁₁!

He quickly knelt down again to look Tommy over, expecting to see where he was hurt. "There's not a mark on him, Catherine!" he said, puzzled.

Woken by their mother's scream, the other boys came running into the room.

"Charles, go next door and ask Mrs Earwaker to come. Tell them mother needs her; as quick as you can!"

The lad seemed to lack understanding and just stood there looking at his young brother lying in his mother's arms.

"Go, lad! *Now, go!*" his father shouted at him.

Isabel, already awake because of the commotion next door, heard frantic banging on the front door.

"Jonathan, something has happened next door! Quickly, get up!"

As Jonathan rushed down the stairs with a candle in his hand, he heard a voice outside calling urgently, "Mrs Earwaker! Mrs Earwaker! Ma needs you!"

"Alright, alright, I'm coming! I'm coming!" Jonathan called out as he unbolted the door. It was the neighbour's eldest boy. "What is it lad?" he asked.

"Pa sent me to get Mrs Earwaker. There's something wrong with Tommy. Ma's crying. Please come!"

Isabel, who had heard what the lad said, already had her coat on over her nightgown. She followed Charles into the house and up the stairs, to see Catherine sitting on the floor in the alcove room with the lifeless little body of Tommy in her arms. Isabel knelt down and put her arm round her, trying to console her.

"What happened, Catherine?"

Between sobs she replied, "He was fine when I put him to bed. I went to check on him and found him like this."

Isabel noticed the blood on his little nightgown. "Has he been hurt by something?" she said, holding up the bloodstained area of his garment.

"It's the first thing I noticed when I saw him," remarked Henry. "But the strange thing is, there is fresh blood on a beam that was above him. How it got there is a mystery to me," he said pointing into the alcove.

Isabel stood up and went closer to look at the beam. "I can't see any blood," she said.

Henry moved the candle closer to the beam. To his shock, she was right. There was no trace of blood on the beam, or of the face. "That's impossible! It was there! I even wiped my fingers over it. He didn't mention anything about the face, as there was now no evidence of it. He looked at his hand. "See, it's still on my fingers!" he said, showing her.

Isabel sensed something was not right. An eerie shiver went through her. She knew she had to take charge of the situation as she could see Henry and Catherine were in a state of shock and the children were crying.

She bent down and said to Catherine, "Let me have Tommy."

Catherine seemed as though she didn't hear as she sat rocking to and fro with him in her arms.

"Catherine, it's all right. I'm just going to put him on the bed," Isabel said as she reached out to take Tommy. Catherine slowly let go of him and Henry helped her to follow Isabel. Catherine sat on the edge of the bed with her head in her hands weeping. Seeing that she was starting to tremble, Isabel put a shawl round her.

"Henry, take the children downstairs with thee, and stoke the fire. I'll bring her down in a while."

Isabel sat down beside Catherine and put her arm round her. All she could hear her say was: "I don't know why! I don't know why!"

"Catherine, we need to get thee downstairs. Ye need to keep warm," she said, helping her up from the bed.

Isabel laid a sheet over Tommy while Catherine stood as though in a trance. As they made their way out of the room, she looked back at her little son, covered on the bed. Isabel gave her a gentle nudge and guided her to the stairs.

"Henry, I know it's late, but I think ye should go and get the priest," Isabel said.

Henry was standing behind Catherine with his arms round her in front of the fire, not responding.

"Henry! Ye need to go and fetch the priest," Isabel repeated.

"Yes, the priest," Henry replied.

1V

The priest was woken by frantic banging on the door. "Alright, alright, I'm coming!" he called out, as the banging continued.

"Sorry, Father Joel, but our boy, Tommy, is dead. I didn't know what to do. Can you come?"

The priest returned to dress and get his bag, while Henry waited outside with the cart. As they travelled, Henry described what had happened since Tommy was put to bed, even the bizarre and mysterious details.

Charles, looking out of the shutters, called out, "They're here!" and rushed to open the door.

"Thanks, Father, for coming out at this hour," said Isabel.

"Where is the lad?" the priest asked.

Henry led the way upstairs and Catherine followed with Isabel behind her.

Uncovering Tommy, the priest saw the mark on his nightshirt.

"I agree. It does look like a handprint," he said, examining the gown.

"That's what I thought. I checked him over but could see no injury on him at all. I cannot, for the life of me, fathom how it got there," said Henry.

"Show me where the lad was lying."

Henry led him into the dimly lit alcove. "Over there against the wall."

The priest felt an uneasiness as he entered but, looking around, could not see any cause for it. "I cannot see how he could have hurt himself in here. It looks fine. The bloodstain must have got on his gown somewhere else. Cover him again and let's go downstairs."

They sat down at the table while Isabel took all the children out of the way to the attic room.

"Henry, Catherine, isn't it?" asked the priest.

"Yes, Father Joel," replied Henry. "What do ye think happened, Father?"

"It's hard to say, especially with children. It's not for us to question when the Lord takes somebody."

"But he was fine, no fever or anything. He was just fine," Catherine sobbed.

"I'm sorry for thy loss. I'll come back tomorrow so that we can discuss burial."

Henry led him out of the door as Isabel came downstairs. "I settled the children. They're fine," she said, putting her arm around Catherine.

"Thank ye for coming, Isabel."

"Not at all. Do ye want me to stay until Henry gets back?"

"No, I'll be alright. Ye had better get back. Thy husband will wonder what has happened to thee."

"If you're sure?"

Jonathan was sitting in front of the fire. "How did it go? I could tell something bad had happened when I saw the priest coming down the track."

"Oh, Jonathan, their youngest boy, Tommy, died. It was awful," she said, clasping his hand.

"How?"

"We don't know. Apparently he was fine when he was put to bed, then when Catherine went to check on him, she found him dead."

"There must have been something wrong with the lad before. People don't just die without a reason," remarked Jonathan. "What did the priest say?"

"I don't know. I was upstairs with the children. The remarkable thing is: there was what looked like a blood-stained handprint on Tommy's nightshirt."

"It's obvious. If there's blood involved, he had to be hurt somewhere, resulting in his death."

"That's the strange thing, Jonathan. There wasn't a mark on him! Also, when I went into the room, I felt a shiver run down my spine."

"That was probably the shock of seeing him lying there."

"No, Jonathan, it was more that. The alcove room had an eerie feel about it. Something was not right, and also I noticed the faint smell of smoke in there."

"Smoke!"

"Yes, like timber burning. But the strangest thing was that Henry said he saw blood on a beam directly over Tommy. When I stood up to look there wasn't anything there, yet he showed me the blood on his fingers where he had touched it."

"Who knows, Isabel; there are many things we don't understand. Only the good Lord knows."

"How did it go, Catherine?" Isabel asked.

"Yes, fine. We have a little place in the corner of the churchyard. The priest said a few words for him. Will ye thank thy husband for making the little wooden cross for him?"

"It's the least we can do. Remember, if ye need me I'm here for thee."

"I'm glad I have such a truly good friend next door, Isabel."

"Has Henry gone back to work?"

"He has to. Life has to go on, especially with all the other children. I must keep busy too, Isabel, if ye know what I mean."

"Of course. I've got so much to do myself. We'll get together again later."

"It's been some time now, Isabel. How are they getting on next door - no more problems with the children?" asked Jonathan.

"As far as I know there haven't been. Catherine hasn't said, and I certainly haven't heard anything."

"What with work and getting home so late, I just don't seem to find the time to talk to them," said Jonathan.

"Don't ye see Henry at work?"

"Nay, the estate is so big. There are a lot of grounds for him to attend. Maybe I'll see him this Sunday at church."

"Let's hope they *are* there this Sunday. They didn't make it last week."

"That's understandable, Isabel, with what they have just gone through."

"Rose is to make her potage again tonight."

"Whatever there is will be fine. Ye have always put a good meal on the table."

"Ye are so easy to please, husband!"

Jonathan turned over to see that his wife was not beside him. "Not again!" he said, seeing Isabel over by the wall. "Come back to bed, woman."

"I can hear a child crying. I pray it hasn't started again, Jonathan."

"It hasn't. It has to be bad dreams. Now come back to bed and let's get some sleep!"

V

Catherine was woken by the girls getting into bed beside her. She automatically put her arms round them, then it dawned on her there were only two of them. "Where's Margaret?" she whispered, so as not to wake her husband.

"She's fast asleep. She didn't see what we did, or hear. It scared us, Ma! There's a face on the wall! And a loud boom of a gun!" one of the girls whispered. "Someone was shouting 'we're burning'," added the other. "It was so frightening, Ma," the girls whispered, knowing if they woke their father it would mean his leather belt.

A sudden chill went through her. She rushed over to the alcove, to see that her fear was justified. There, against the wall, was Margaret. By the pale look of her, she knew it had happened again.

Henry was woken by screaming. He could see Catherine with her back to him in the alcove doorway. He rushed over and squeezed past her to see Margaret lying there, apparently lifeless. In desperate hope, he bent to feel her forehead but the icy coldness of it confirmed that

45

she was indeed dead. To add to his horror, he could see the same bloody handprint on her gown! Instinctively, he looked up at the wall beam and saw the face again, with blood seeping from the wood and running down the wall. This time the face appeared to be grinning at him; then suddenly both the face and blood vanished before his eyes.

As Isabel got back into bed she heard harrowing screams coming though the wall. She knew it was Catherine and, by the loudness of it, she knew that it was one of the children again.

"Ye had better go," said Jonathan.

Isabel hurriedly put her shawl around her and rushed next door.

One of the eldest boys opened the door for her and, giving him a light hug, she rushed upstairs.

"Isabel, it's Margaret. She's dead!" cried Catherine.

"Oh God, not again, Catherine!" Isabel said putting both arms around her. "Henry, ye will have to go and get the priest again. I'll look after things here."

Henry took one more anguished look at the child lying there as he went out of the door.

"Catherine, help me to lift Margaret and put her on thy bed," Isabel said softly.

As Isabel went into the alcove room, her eyes were drawn to the same bloody handprint on Margaret's gown as there had been on Tommy's and a shiver ran through her. Picking her up gently, they laid her on the bed and covered her.

"Catherine, we have to go downstairs. Henry will be back with the priest soon," Isabel said, as she helped her out of the room.

"Where are the girls?" Catherine asked.

"The eldest lad took them upstairs with the others. They're fine," Isabel replied as they made their way downstairs.

Henry stood outside the priest's door, concerned about waking him up again, but he knew he had to. The creaking, heavy oak door of the building opened.

A sleepy voice said, "Yes, what is it?"

"It's Henry Derwin, Father. Can ye come? It's my little Margaret, she's dead."

"Henry Derwin," the priest muttered as though wondering where he'd heard that name before. Then he remembered. "Ah, Henry! Ye lost a lad a little while ago?"

"Yes, Father - Tommy. Now Margaret. Can ye come?"

"Give me a minute to get changed."

The door opened and Henry came in, followed by the priest. Catherine stood up and gave Henry a hug.

"Sorry, Father Joel, for making thee come out again," Catherine said.

The priest gave Catherine's hand a gentle squeeze. "Where is she?" he asked.

"Upstairs - the same place as before," Henry replied as he led the way.

The priest uncovered the child and could see by the ashen colour of her face that the life force had been drained from her. As he was about to recover her, his eyes were drawn to a red stain on her gown. He tweaked the folds to reveal a blood-stained handprint.

"Where was she found?" he asked.

"Over in the alcove room behind thee," Henry replied.

As the priest entered, a sudden chill went through him. He had known such a feeling before and knew that a presence was in the room. Turning around he said to Henry, "I need thee to take everyone downstairs now. I have some work to do up here. Whatever ye hear or whatever takes place, **do not enter this room."**

Nobody questioned his authority, and they did as he had said.

The priest closed the door behind them and went back into the candle-lit alcove room. Taking out of his bag a container of salt and a tumbler of holy water, he started to pray the prayer of exorcism and began sprinkling the holy water around the room.

As his prayers intensified, a deep, menacing voice said, "Jesus I know, but *thee* I don't!" The priest immediately clasped the rosary cross around his neck, then his eyes were drawn to the appearance of a face and smouldering ember on a beam along the outside wall. As he started to take the lid off the tumbler of salt, the glowing ember burst into flame, and began to fill the room with smoke. As hard as it was for him to breathe, he had to finish the prayer if he was to put whatever it was to rest. He knew he had a battle on his hands as his prayers were almost drowned by a husky voice saying, "Cursed be thee, Derwin, and thy descendants!"

There was a pause and then he heard the voices of panic-stricken men shouting, "We're burning! We're going down!" A piercing scream and what he saw next put a halt to his prayers. It was the appearance of a bloody handprint on the beam with blood oozing from it, and starting to run down the wall.

As he stood there mesmerized, there was a loud explosion that blew him backwards out of the alcove and slammed the door shut. Then silence filled the room. As he lay there, he felt that his life had been nearly drained from him. Shaken and weak, he got to his feet, and slowly opened the door to peer into the room. As he did, he saw the handprint vanishing back into the beam. He closed the door on the alcove room, and made his way downstairs.

As he entered, they all stood up and gasped, for the priest's face and clothes were blackened by smoke.

"Are ye all right, Father Joel?" Henry asked anxiously.

"I need to sit down," the priest said, staggering to a chair.

"Ye look like thee could do with a hot drink," Catherine said, going over to the range.

"Have ye got something a little stronger?" he asked.

"Sorry, Father Joel, we don't," Henry replied, a little shocked that a priest should ask for such.

The priest groped in his bag and produced a small silver flask, drank from it, and put it back in his bag. Henry could tell, by the smell of it, that it was the 'stronger stuff' he had been referring to.

As they all stood looking at him, Father Joel said, "What do ye know of the cottage?"

"Nothing really. We haven't long been moved in. Why, Father? Is there something we need to know?" asked Henry.

"Don't know yet, but one thing I do know is there's something not right in that alcove upstairs." He didn't reveal to them the true extent of what he had just experienced, so as not to scare them; his appearance had been alarming enough.

"I sensed something wrong when I went in there earlier. A chill went through my bones," Isabel said.

The priest looked at her, but didn't say anything.

"Father Joel, are ye saying that whatever was in that room was the reason for the children dying?" Catherine asked.

"I can't say for sure. Look, it's late. Let me do some enquiries about the building of this place. It's more

49

important to get the arrangements done to bury the child. Meanwhile, don't go into that room, and especially don't let the children sleep in there."

Catherine looked at Henry. Turning to face the priest she said, "I wouldn't have put them in there, even if ye hadn't said that!"

The priest stood up and started for the door, followed by Henry.

"I'll be back tomorrow to arrange the burial."

"Thank thee, Father Joel, Catherine said, as they went out.

"What are we going to do, Isabel? I should have known something was wrong the first night when the children started screaming and saying they heard voices. If I had done something then, Tommy and Margaret might still be alive!" Catherine said, wretchedly.

"Ye couldn't have known, Catherine. It could have been, as thy husband said, that it was a new place and that they would have eventually settled down."

"But ..."

"Nay 'buts', Catherine! Ye cannot blame thyself. I'll stay with thee until thy husband gets back. My husband will be wondering what has happened to me. I will come round tomorrow to see how ye are doing."

"I don't know what I'd have done without thee," Catherine said.

V1

Isabel crept upstairs, trying not to wake her husband.

"I'm not asleep," he said. "What happened?"

"It was their girl, Margaret. She's dead! There's something not right next door; I can sense it. My mother, and her mother before her, had the gift of knowing. It's been in our family for generations. I can understand an illness, but not just dying for no reason at all. Another thing - they died in the same room."

"Ye shouldn't talk like that, Isabel. Ye know how superstitious people are. I confess it sounds strange, but it could be a coincidence," said Jonathan. "What did the priest say? I take it he did come?"

"Yes, Henry went to get him. It was his appearance when he came downstairs, and the look on his face, that said something was wrong. His face and clothes were black, as if he had been in a house fire! He told them that they mustn't go in that room, and went on to ask who built the cottages, to which we replied that we didn't know. By the urgency in his voice it seemed important that he should find out."

"I know who it was, Isabel: Samuel Wright. I was talking to him on my first day at work; he's the builder on the estate. Apparently he knew that I was living in one of the cottages he had built and asked me how we were faring in it. I told him it was fine, and then he asked which one was our dwelling. I told him the left one. It was the way he said, "Good!". At the time I thought that was a strange answer; it was as if to imply that there was something wrong with the other one."

"Didn't ye ask him if there was?" Isabel asked.

"Nay, ye can't stand around talking; we were both busy," replied Jonathan.

"It sounds as if something is definitely wrong. Do ye think I should tell Henry and Catherine about it?"

"Nay, we don't know anything for sure. Leave it to the priest - it will be better coming from him when he finds out a bit more. I'll tell him Sunday what I know; it will save him asking around."

"Apparently he's coming back tomorrow to see them. Do ye want me to tell him who the builder was?"

"Ye might as well," replied Jonathan.

"Ma! The priest is coming down the track!" the eldest boy called through the door.

"Go quickly and find thy Pa! He's somewhere up the copes."

Opening the door, Catherine said, "Good morrow, Father Joel. So sorry ye have to come out; I know ye must be very busy. My husband won't be long; he knows ye are here. Will ye take a seat?"

"How are ye both bearing up Catherine?" Father Joel asked as he sat down at the table.

"It was dreadful losing Tommy, and now Margaret. It's so hard, Father. It's the not knowing why - especially as they were well," she replied.

52

"Sorry to keep thee waiting, Father. There's so much to do out there," Henry said as he rushed in.

"Not at all Henry. I was just asking how ye both are bearing up?"

"The amount of work helps. Father Joel, can I ask: is there something in that room that we should know about? It's just that I sensed ye were keeping things back from us," asked Henry.

"As I said yesterday, until I find out more about the cottage, I cannot say for sure. I'm here to talk about the burial. I know last time ye paid for the gravedigger. Because of the expense, do ye want to dig the grave thyself?"

"If that's all right, Father, as money is tight, especially with me not working today."

"Come to the graveyard and get it prepared today. I can do the service tomorrow. We need to get her buried as soon as possible," said the priest. "Where is the girl now?"

"She's still upstairs in our room," replied Henry.

Heading for the stairs, Father Joel said, "I need to say a few prayers over her. There's no need to come with me." He said that as an excuse to have another look in the alcove room.

He could see the girl's body lying covered in the corner of the main room but in front of him was the door to the alcove. Slowly he unlatched it and, as he pulled it towards him, it made a creaking sound. Cautiously, he stayed outside just peering in. It looked normal and quiet. Even the beam where he had seen the glowing ember and blood looked normal.

"Are ye all right, Father Joel?" Henry called up the stairs, breaking the silence.

"Aye – I'll be down in a while," the priest replied.

As he turned with his back to the alcove room, he felt a shiver go down his spine. He closed the door hurriedly and went downstairs.

Because Catherine noticed a look of concern on his face she said, "Is everything all right, Father?"

"Aye, everything is fine. I'll see thee on the morrow at the church," he said as he made his way out.

"Thank thee, Father Joel!" Henry called out after him.

"He seemed to be in rather a hurry to go, didn't he?" Catherine remarked.

"He's probably got a lot to do, Catherine."

Looking out of the shutters, Isabel saw the priest getting ready to mount his horse and hurried outside. "Father Joel, do ye have a minute?" she said. "I have some information about who built the cottages."

"Oh aye," the priest replied.

"My husband was talking to the builder on the A'aeth Estate where he works. It turns out that *he* built the cottages. Apparently he asked my husband which cottage we lived in. When he told him it was the left one, he replied, "Good." My husband seemed to think that his answer indicated that there was perhaps something wrong with the other one."

"Very interesting. I will have a chat with him. Thank thee, Mrs ....?"

"Earwaker. Isabella Earwaker."

Squire A'aeth ambled down the drive on his horse. Stopping, he said, "Good morrow to thee, Father Joel! We don't often see thee here on the estate. What can I do for thee?"

"Good morrow to thee, Squire A'aeth. Aye, we don't often see thee either in the church," he said smiling.

"Sorry to be a bother - I am looking for the builder Samuel Wright."

"Samuel Wright? Oh aye, I think he's up at the coach house - left at the house, around the back. What's he been up to; nothing bad I hope? I only have God-fearing men working for me here, Father," the Squire said.

"Nay. I've been told he can help me with one or two questions I need answering," replied the priest.

"Then by thy leave, Father Joel" he said and rode off.

The priest found his way to the coach house, to see two men up on the roof.

"Samuel Wright!" the priest called. Samuel stopped working when he heard his name and looked down to see the priest looking up at him.

"What have ye been up to, Samuel?" his friend, Benjamin, said jokingly.

"Aye, Father, that would be me. What can I do for thee?"

"Can ye stop for a while? I need a word with thee?" called Father Joel

"I am due a break. Allow me a minute and I'll be down," replied Samuel.

As Samuel approached the priest, he was thinking that maybe he wanted some work done on the church. He said, "Now, Father, how can I help thee?"

"I hear that ye built the two cottages up on the downs. I'm looking for a little information about them."

"Aye, that is true, and fine cottages they be. What do ye want to know?" Samuel asked.

"I heard that ye were talking to Jonathan Earwaker about them and used the word 'Good!' when he said he lived in the left one. To me that would indicate that there was possibly something wrong with the other one. Is there?"

"I'm not too sure what ye mean, Father. I built it as well as the other. Why would ye follow such a line of questioning, about a mere word that I used?"

"I have been called out twice now to the Derwin's, the other cottage. Two of their young children have died in a short space of time, both in strange circumstances."

"What do ye mean, '*strange circumstances*', Father?"

"They were healthy children when they were put to bed yet they died in their sleep - both in the same room."

"What room would that be then?" Samuel asked.

"A little alcove room, upstairs, next to the fire place," replied the priest.

Samuel's face looked concerned. "Ye say an alcove room upstairs? If I remember well, there are only two rooms up there: an attic above and a bedroom - no other room, except for a small storage area in the bedroom. Is that what ye are calling 'the alcove room'?"

"Aye that would be it. The Derwins used that to sleep some of the children. It was there that they died. The reason I'm asking is: when I went in there, something of an evil presence was there. I wanted to know if, when ye built the cottage, there was anything untoward about the place?"

Samuel hesitated with his answer. "Nay... not that I can remember."

"Are ye sure?" asked the priest.

"Aye, I'm sure. If that's all, Father, then, by thy leave, I have to get back to work."

The priest, who knew he was not telling the truth, mounted his horse and rode off.

"I couldn't help overhearing what the priest was asking thee, Samuel. Why didn't ye tell him about the lad dying there?" asked Benjamin.

"Nay, Benjamin, best left alone. I don't want to be blamed for the deaths of the children; the grief of the parents could cause a lot of trouble for me. They'll be looking for someone to blame. Best left alone."

"I don't know, Samuel. What if it happens again?" replied Benjamin.

"As I said, Benjamin, best left alone. We've got work to do."

V11

Benjamin watched the priest outside welcoming people in to the Sunday service.

"Morning, Father. Benjamin Miles," he said, shaking his hand. Can I be having a quick word with thee after the service?"

"Aye, of course - if ye hold back till everyone has gone."

"Now, Benjamin Miles, what is it ye want to talk about?"

"Ye came to the A'aeth estate the other day to talk to Samuel Wright, asking about the cottages. I couldn't help overhearing the conversation. Samuel didn't tell thee all. I was there helping to build them, when it happened."

"What do ye mean, '*when it happened*'? What happened?" asked the priest.

"A young lad died. Went by the name of Harry ...... ; sorry, Father, I forget his surname. He was Samuel's apprentice, a hard working lad. He lived in the village and was doing well at learning the trade . . ."

"The lad! What happened to him?" the priest interrupted impatiently.

"Oh, aye. He was told to pass up a beam for the upper room that Samuel and I were working on. He was half way up the ladder when he screamed and fell backwards, with the beam falling on him. It killed him outright; messy business it was. But the strange thing was: as we lifted the beam off him there was a handprint in blood on his chest! There was no rhyme or reason how it got there, but after we took the lad home to his mother, we went back to carry on with the work. It was then we noticed the beam had what looked like an evil face and the number thirteen carved on it. I told Samuel it was cursed, and no good would come of it if he used it."

"How did he answer?" asked the priest.

"He said that if he didn't .... ." Benjamin stopped suddenly. He was a simple, superstitious man, and had been racked with guilt for not speaking up about what he knew. The deaths of the children had tormented him and telling the priest was the only way he could think of to attain peace. His conscience had overridden his loyalty to Samuel, yet now he was beginning to fear the consequences. He might not have any work from Samuel again, for one thing.

"If he didn't - what?" pressed Father Joel.

Benjamin's mind groped for words to answer the priest without condemning Samuel. If he told him the truth, Samuel's reputation as a trustworthy builder would be finished, and Squire A'aeth would not want anyone working for him that had scandal attached to him. His thoughts were interrupted by the priest saying, "Benjamin! This is important, man! Answer me!"

"Err...... If he didn't use the beam, it would cost him two days and he wouldn't be finished on time."

"Are ye saying he *used* it?" asked the priest incredulously.

"Aye, Father," replied Benjamin sheepishly.

"Why didn't ye stop him?"

"I couldn't. I only work for him when he needs me. I did say that it was cursed and no good would come of using it. It's nothing to do with me, Father."

"Do ye know where I can find Samuel?"

"That depends, Father, on when ye might be seeking him. If it were now, he would be in the Black Dog having a few ales; after that most likely sleeping it off at his place."

"And where might that be?"

"He has a yard just outside the village but, as I said Father, he will be sleeping."

"Ye did the right thing coming to me. Fare thee well, Benjamin. I have work to do."

Samuel was woken by insistent knocking at his door but, as he was reluctant to be disturbed during his Sunday afternoon sleep, he decided to ignore it.

"Samuel Wright!" he heard, "It's Father Joel. I need to speak to thee!"

The only reason the priest would want to speak to him was about the cottages again. Samuel laid there hoping he would go away but he knew, by the sternness in his voice, that wasn't going to happen.

"Samuel Wright! I know ye are in there! I am not going away until ye open this door!" the priest said, knocking more loudly.

Samuel knew he had no choice but to face him. "Wait a minute!" he snapped as he made his way to the door.

"Don't ye know it's a sin to lie?" the priest bellowed at him, pushing his way past Samuel into his home. "Why didn't ye tell me about the lad dying when the cottage was being built, and the beam with the number on?"

"What number?" asked Samuel, shrinking back from him.

"I know all about it! The number thirteen carved on the beam, that cursed beam that killed the lad, and now two more have died because of it! Ye knew it was cursed, yet ye put profit first. Ye are an evil man, Samuel Wright. May God forgive thee, although I don't know if the parents will, when they find out!"

Samuel stood there, lost for words. His head was aching from too much ale, and the priest shouting at him was making it worse.

"What have ye to say for thyself?" the priest demanded.

"Err, uh."

"Speak up, man! Where did ye get the timbers from?"

"From Pike's salvage yard. Pike said they were from the ships that went down. I remember him saying the Cordellere's powder kegs blew up, taking the Regent with it. Most of the crew either drowned or were burnt to death. The lucky ones died in the explosion, but how could what happened at sea cause death now?"

"Those beams ye used were from the disaster, or for sure one was, and from what I can make out, it was the one that had been marked with the face and number thirteen, a cursed number," replied the priest.

"Well, how it could cause death is beyond me! I know the number thirteen is thought to bring bad luck, and the look of a face in the beam did shock me at first; but I reckoned it to be just the grain in the wood. If I had known it would cause death I would never have used it. I thought the lad just fell off the ladder. Ye have to believe me, Father! I give thee my word!"

"Didn't ye think something was amiss when ye saw the handprint on the lad? That alone should have told thee. Nay, Samuel Wright, ye put profit before life!"

"How do ye know about the handprint?" asked Samuel, shocked.

"Benjamin Miles told me everything."

"Benjamin!" replied Samuel, sardonically.

"Aye, at least he doesn't lie. But ye, Samuel Wright, are a liar! Now, tell me, where do I find Pike's yard?"

"It's on the estuary."

Father Joel marched out without another word.

"Good morrow to ye, Father. What can I do for thee?"

"I've come to find a man called 'Pike'."

"That would be me."

"Do ye know a man called Samuel Wright, who apparently purchased some timbers from thee?"

"Well now, Father, ye say 'Samuel Wright'? Let me think. My old mind ain't as sharp as it used to be. Usually it needs a little something to take away the fogginess."

The priest, taking from his saddlebag a bottle of wine, said, "Maybe this will help?"

"That be kindly of thee, Father! I'll let my men have that, as I don't drink the devil's brew."

"No, of course ye don't. Now - Samuel Wright?"

"Aye, I know Samuel Wright. I've had dealings with him – he's bought many a timber from me for some years now," Pike answered.

"The timbers I was referring to were for the cottages for Squire A'aeth."

"Aye, I remember. I was thinking at the time that he'd done well, working for the Squire. Would there be a problem with the timbers? I only sell the best oak here, and don't ye let any man tell thee otherwise," Pike said with a concerned look on his face.

"Samuel Wright tells me that the timbers came from the sunken Regent. Would that be true?"

"T'is to the best of my knowledge they did, as there were only two wrecks at the time - the Regent and the Cordellere."

"How do ye know it wasn't the Cordellere?"

"I knows my oak. The timbers he had were the best English oak, apart from the ones he scrounged off me that I was going to burn."

"Pray tell me of those that ye felt ye should burn?"

"As I told thee, I am a man for selling the best oak and they was only fit for burning, as they be short bits of broken timbers. Some 'ad been burnt in the battle, but he was keen on 'aving them. So I let him 'ave them, and cheap they was."

"I take it ye have been around here for some time and have heard a lot of tales?" Father Joel asked.

"Aye, not a lot of talk gets past my ears! But ye say 'tales'. What sort of 'tales' would ye be wanting to know about?"

"Anything about the Regent - when it was being built, any superstitious talk or rumours of curses. Things like that."

"Ah, now Father, people round 'ere pays for a good curse tale. A tale of the King's ship is worth a piece of silver."

"Look man! I've given ye all that ye are going to get out of me. Unless ye want to be damned, ye will tell me what I want to know!"

"I'm only an honest man, trying to make a few pennies 'ere and there, Father. Aye, as it 'appens, there is a tale of the timbers that were used on the Regent. Rumour 'as it that a certain oak beam came from old Tobias Spry's place. He 'ad a place in the woods not far from 'ere. He kept himself to himself, never mixing with the village folk.

Some say he practised in the dark arts, and all sorts could be heard coming from his shack. People wouldn't go near 'is place, 'specially at night.

Then, when animals started to disappear and sickness came upon the village, they said he was the cause of it, but what made the village folk get angry was the disappearance of a child, Henrietta Derwin. Her father, Daniel Derwin, gathered the villagers together and went to 'is place, armed with clubs and pitchforks. Banging on 'is door, they demanded 'im to come out with the child. They say Spry was heard saying that he didn't know anything about the child and wanted to be left alone, but the angry crowd weren't 'aving any of it and forced the door open.

Daniel Derwin and one other went in; they could see the walls and floor covered in symbols of triangles, pentagrams, heads of animals and bones, but no child. Looking around, their eyes was drawn towards the oak beam over the fire that 'ad an image of an evil face entwined in the grain o' the wood, with the number thirteen carved into it. "This is the proof we need!" one of the men said to 'im.

Daniel Derwin, who was a big man, took 'old of him single-'anded and tried to make 'im confess to where the child was, but he denied taking the child. They say that while the other man 'eld one of his 'ands to a beam above the fire, Daniel Derwin drove a spike through it, fixing 'im to the beam. They left 'im there and went back outside, closing the door and shouting: "There's evil in there! Stay back!"

"Burn the place!" Daniel Derwin commanded. The crowd was soon in a frenzy and started shouting out: "Burn him!" The place was soon in flames. It's said that, in desperation to get out of the shack, he must 'ave pulled 'is hand off the spike to get to the door. But, as he tried to get out, he was prodded back into the flames with the pitchforks. It was then he could be seen, standing there all in flames, screaming, "Cursed be thee, Daniel Derwin, and all thy descendants *and* the village!" as he burned alive. It wasn't long before all that was left was a pile of ashes - of him and most of 'is place.

Some weeks later, the shipbuilders' men were sent into the woods to fell oak trees, and came across the burnt remains of the shack. Seeing that amongst all the burnt timbers there was one almost untouched by the flames, they decided to take it."

"Was it the oak beam with the face on it?" the priest asked.

"Because it was the only beam not burned up by the fire, I'd say it was. Those men didn't even inspect it. If they 'ad they would 'ave seen the evil in it and left it there. But nay, they were so lax in their work, they took the cursed beam with them to be a part of the Regent, and the cursed beam took that ship down to the bottom of the sea. What say ye of that tale, Father? Will ye not consider that piece of silver?"

"So how much of that tale is true?" asked Father Joel.

"It be as true as my name is 'Pike'! What comes out of my mouth is always the truth, Father."

The priest gave him a disbelieving look, mounted his horse and rode off, with Pike calling out to him, "So will ye not consider that piece of silver then?"

On his way back to the church he pondered over Pike's tale. *Was it plausible enough to explain the evil in the cottage?* Something inside told him it was, and now he knew what he had to do.

VIII

"Ma! The priest is here again!" Catherin's eldest said, rushing through the door.

Catherine looked out of the shutters to see the priest dismounting his horse.

Opening the door, she said, "Good morrow, Father Joel. What brings thee out here?"

"Good morrow to thee, Catherine. I wanted to catch thee this morning after church to see if I could come this afternoon, but ye had left before I had a chance to speak to thee."

"Come in, Father. Pray take a seat," Catherine said. "What is it ye want to talk about?"

"Have ye had any more trouble with the children being disturbed at night?" he asked her.

"Nay, Father Joel, not since we lost Marg . . ." she said, unable to finish saying her name. "The girls sleep in with us now and we've kept that door shut since."

"Good!" replied the priest.

"Father, we asked thee before, is there something in that room that we should know about? Only if there were,

66

I don't think I could live in such a place. I think it would finish me if I were to lose another child."

"All I can tell thee is what I've found out. It has something to do with the materials the builder used in the room. I don't think ye have to concern thyself too much with it, as long as ye keep the door shut and don't go in there. But I'm more interested in finding out why a beam could leave a force in that room that can take the life of your children."

"So there is something in there?" asked Catherine anxiously.

"As I said, I think as long as ye keep the children out of there, it will be fine. Do ye mind if I take another look at the room? There's something I need to do."

"Do what ye have to, Father," replied Catherine.

Father Joel made his way upstairs. He stood outside the door and took out of his bag a small silver cross, a hammer and nail. He opened the door and walked into a heavy and depressing atmosphere. He could feel the weight of suffocating fear, despair and a sense of hopelessness coming upon him. He attempted to shake it off as he started to recite an exorcism prayer from the small scroll: *"In nomine Domini Iesu Christi, Dei et Domini. Nos Adjutorium nostrum in nomine Domini omnis satanica viribus a spiritibus immundis: Omnia impium legiones in unum et omnes invadentes infernali fiunt. Ab insidiis diabliand."*

Having finished the prayer, he faced the beam and was about to hammer the cross into it but suddenly his attention was drawn to the face in the grain, which seemed to turn and grin at him. Then the door behind him slammed shut. He knew that the evil in the room would do all it could to distract him from doing what he had to do. A smouldering ember appeared on the beam and the room began to fill with smoke, while blood starting to ooze from the beam and run down the wall. The priest somehow knew he must not let the blood touch him. He took the cross and positioned it, then, with the other hand, he lifted the hammer to nail it in, but a force held his arm back.

"**Ye foul evil spirit!**" he said at the top of his voice. "**Ye will not stop me!**" With all his strength, he hammered it in. A piercing scream filled the room, followed by blood that came spurting out from around the nail. The priest stepped back in time to stop it going on him. He could see the smoke disappearing, along with the blood, and could feel the heavy atmosphere in the room lifting. The door slowly started to open on its own.

He knew it was over. He had put whatever it was to rest. He went out and closed the door behind him. He took out his small knife and scratched on the door the words: '𝕰nter an𝔡 𝔟e 𝕯ame𝔡íous', then tied the latch with a cord. As he was about to head downstairs, he realised that he had dropped his scroll in the room, but rather than go back in he decided to leave it there.

Catherine had been outside fetching water and was busying herself over the fire as Father Joel came into the room. "Everything alright, Father?" she asked.

"Aye, it is now. I don't think ye have anything further to be concerned about, but I still wouldn't use the room. If ye value thy soul, keep it closed and do not enter it."

"Thanks, Father Joel. I assure thee, we won't!"

"Well, I'd better get going. Don't forget - keep that door closed!" said the priest.

"Fare thee well, Father Joel," Catherine said, closing the door.

Isabel saw the priest leaving from her window. "Rose, look after the children," she said, and went next door to speak to Catherine. "Is everything alright? I saw Father Joel leaving."

"Aye, it is now. He came to have another look in the room upstairs. And, whatever he did, he says we won't have any more problems in the house."

"What did he do?"

"I don't know, but his words were stern that we should never go in there and must keep the door shut," replied Catherine.

"How are ye going to stop the children? Ye know what they are like," said Isabel.

"Do ye think the builder would board up the door?" asked Catherine.

"I don't know. I think ye would have to ask Squire A'aeth," Isabel replied.

"Aye, I'll speak to Henry tonight."

"I'm glad it's all over for thee, Catherine."

"As am I, Isabel! I was saying to Father Joel that I couldn't stand losing another child and that we could not stay if it were to happen again."

"I should hate to lose such a good friend, Catherine, but now it's all over ye won't have to leave," Isabel said, grasping her hand.

"I think we will always be good friends, wherever we are. It's as though it was meant to be," Catherine said.

"That's a lovely thing to say, Catherine. Yes, always good friends, forever."

"Evening, Pa," Rose said. Ma's upstairs with the others. Sit thee down, Pa. Food won't be long."

"Smells nice, Rose! Ye will make a good wife some day," Jonathan said.

He ate with a hearty appetite, finishing as Isabel came into the room and Rose headed for the stairs.

"Ye taught her well, Isabel. She's become a young woman and will be a good catch for someone. Just like thee when we met."

"What do ye need mending?"

"Nothing. Can't a husband say nice things about his wife?"

Isabel put her hand on his shoulder. "Come sit by the fire. I will get thy pipe, and ye can tell me about the day."

Not much to tell. It's been the same as usual - mending and cleaning the carriages. How's thy day been?"

"Father Joel paid a visit next door."

"Problems again?"

"No. Catherine said he had put to rest the problem, but told her to keep the door closed and never use the room again. She is thinking of getting Henry to ask for permission to get the room boarded up. Do ye think the Squire will agree to it?"

I should imagine it'll not be done for nothing. I'd offer to do it myself but, if the Squire found out, it could mean losing my job and our home. I'll tell ye what, I helped Samuel Wright out the other day so he owes me a favour. I'll have a word with him to see if he will do it. If I catch Henry in the morning I'll tell him."

"That's good of thee, husband. I suspect he hasn't got much money, especially after the burials of his young ones."

IX

"Morning, Henry. I was hoping to catch you. The wife was telling me that ye intend to have the room boarded up."

"Morning, Jonathan. Yes, but it will cost money I don't have, and even if I did, I don't know if the Squire will allow it."

"Why don't ye let me have a word with Samuel Wright?" said Jonathan.

"Isn't he the builder who's working on the coach house?"

"That's him. He owes me a favour. I'm sure he would do it on the side, without involving the Squire. I'll ask him if ye wish?"

"That's kindly of thee, Jonathan."

"It shouldn't take him long - especially as he knows the cottage."

"Why is that?" asked Henry.

"Didn't ye know he built the place?" replied Jonathan.

"No. So he's the builder Father Joel was going to talk to. Father told Catherine the problem might have something to do with the materials used. If I find out he's the reason I lost Tommy and Margaret, he will hang for it or I will!" Henry said angrily.

Ye don't know for sure, Henry, that it was his fault. Wait until I ask him if he will come and do the job – let's see what his reaction is. Who knows, if he is harbouring guilt, it might make him want to make amends by doing the job for nothing. No, let him come here, then we can confront him."

"So be it, Jonathan, but I tell thee he'll not get away with it if he is in some way responsible," replied Henry.

"Morning, Samuel, all alone today?" asked Jonathan.

"Aye, me and that 'so called friend' had a falling out. To think of all the work I've given him!" Samuel grunted.

"You mean Benjamin? What's he done then?"

"He talks too much! That's all I got to say on the matter. I got work to do and twice as much now I'm on my own."

"Can I have a word with thee, maybe in thy break?" asked Jonathan.

"If I find time to stop," replied Samuel peevishly.

Jonathan headed for the horse and cart to set off home. Samuel hadn't found time to stop so they hadn't spoken but, just as he was about to climb up on his cart, he heard: "Ye wanted to speak with me?" It was Samuel walking towards him.

"That was a long, hard day," replied Jonathan.

"No choice when ye are working alone. I need to get to the tavern for a jug of ale! What is it ye want then?" asked Samuel.

"My neighbour, Henry Derwin, needs some work done at the cottage - a door boarded up. I was hoping that I could call on that favour, in asking thee to do the work for him, without involving the Squire."

"Isn't he the head gardener here?"

"Aye, he is that."

"And ye say he lives in the cottage next to thee?"

"Aye, is that a problem?" Jonathan asked, waiting to see his reaction.

There was a long pause from Samuel. "Ye say it's a door to be boarded up? Would it be the little room upstairs, off the main room?

"Aye. Apparently, they don't want the children going in there. Will ye do it?"

"Tell him I'll call after work tomorrow. Make sure he doesn't say anything to the Squire about it. The least the Squire knows, the better all round."

"How much would the charge be?"

"As ye say, Jonathan, I owe thee a favour," replied Samuel.

"Then I'll say goodnight to thee, Samuel."

"A long day again?" Isabel asked as Jonathan came in, looking tired.

"Aye, I got delayed with Samuel Wright - asking if he would do the boarding-up next door."

"Shouldn't ye have spoken to Henry about it first?" Isabel asked.

"I did, this morning. Do ye know, he wasn't aware it was Samuel Wright that built the cottages?"

"What did he say when ye told him?"

"He was angry, saying all sorts of daft things. I calmed him down, and told him to let me deal with it."

"Was he happy with that?"

"He was when I said I was hoping to get it done for nothing".

"So what did Samuel Wright say when ye asked him?"

"When I told him it was for my neighbour, he went quiet. And, by the look on his face, I swear, Isobel, he

73

knew about the goings-on in that room. He couldn't wait to come and do the work - I suspect it was guilt tearing at him. I know *I* couldn't have that on my conscience. Also he knows that, if the Squire finds out, he'll be finished."

"So when is he coming?" asked Isabel.

"Tomorrow night, after work. I'll go next door after supper and tell Henry."

"Do ye think there will be trouble with Henry?"

"Not at first. If he has a head on his shoulders, he'll let him do the work first."

"I hope so, Jonathan. It's the last thing Catherine will want, her husband being taken away," said Isabel, worried.

"It won't come to that — I'll make sure of it. We wouldn't want a pretty thing like thee being concerned," Jonathan said, smiling. "Now where's my supper?"

"Ye are an old charmer, husband!" she said, hugging him.

"Food, woman! Food!"

After work Jonathan went over to the coach house. Samuel was there packing his tools away. "Are ye still on for tonight, Samuel?"

"Aye, I said I'd be there. If I *say* I'll do it, I *will*! I'm a man of my word. But first I'm having one or two jugs of ale at the tavern," Samuel said, irritated by the tone in Jonathan's voice.

"Ye misunderstand me, sir. I was only asking if ye will be there tonight. It doesn't matter to me one way or the other. I was going to give thee a hand with the work, but with that attitude, I don't think I will," said Jonathan.

"I don't need anyone's help. Tell Derwin I'll be there later."

74

"Usual, Samuel?" Dan, the innkeeper, enquired as the weary builder slumped onto a seat.

"Aye, I be needing it tonight!"

"Ye have the look of a man with trouble upon his shoulders," said Dan, putting the jug on the table.

"Nay, not I. It's been a long day and I'm not finished yet. I just need a quiet drink before I set off again," replied Samuel.

"Then I'll be leaving thee to it," the innkeeper said.

Henry stepped through the doors of the inn. He felt he needed a drink before going home and facing Samuel Wright.

"I haven't seen thee for a while, Henry," the innkeeper said, "but, by the look of thee, I'd say ye will be needing a jug or two."

"Aye, Dan. I need an ale to calm me, before going home," he replied.

"Problem with the wife?"

"Nay, nothing like that. It's somebody's actions that's making me angry."

"Anger is it? That can cause a man to do all sorts of things he wouldn't normally do - I've seen a lot of it in here with fights. I say that ye had best keep that anger out of here and take it home with thee," said the innkeeper.

"Ye will be having no trouble from me. I'm here for a drink only, then I'll be on my way," he replied.

Henry sat down, sipping his ale. As he looked around he noticed a man that he thought was Samuel Wright, sitting in the corner. He had only seen him once at the estate, and had never spoken to him. Without thinking, he got up and went over to his table.

"Would ye be Samuel Wright?" Henry said to him.

"Aye. Who's asking? State thy business, sir."

75

"Henry Derwin. I hear it's because of thee my young ones died," he said loudly, standing over him.

Samuel didn't say anything. He was more concerned that everyone in the inn was looking at him.

"What do ye say for thyself, Samuel Wright, ye child murderer?" Henry said raising his voice even more.

"Ye mistake me, man! I've never murdered any child. Everyone here knows I wouldn't do such a thing!"

"Liar!" Henry shouted at him.

"Keep thy voice down, friend, and have a drink with me. We have things to talk about," Samuel said, trying to calm him down.

His words enraged Henry even more. Tipping over the table and grabbing him by the throat, he said, "I'm no friend of thee, after what ye have done to my family!"

"Let him go, Henry!" the innkeeper said with his hand on Henry's shoulder. "I'll be having no fighting in here. Take it outside!"

"I only came in for a quiet drink. I don't want any trouble," said Samuel.

Henry let him go and backed off. "I'm not finished with thee. I'll see that ye get what's coming to thee!" he snarled at him, as he made his way out of the inn.

The innkeeper lifted the table back up and said to Samuel, "What's he talking about? What's all this about murdered children?"

"I ain't murdered no children! The man's mistaken me for someone else. I ain't never seen him before," replied Samuel.

"That may be, but I know Henry. He'd not behave like that if he didn't have reason to."

"I tell you, I ain't seen him before, or his children."

Samuel sat there trying to avoid the stares of those who were talking and looking his way. "Another jug over here!" he called out to Dan. After several more jugs of

76

ale, he stood up, staggered out of the door and made his way home.

X

"What happened to thee last night? One too many?" asked Jonathan.

"Nay, the drink's not the problem. So ye haven't spoken with Henry Derwin then?" replied Samuel.

"Nay, I don't think he came home at his usual time. I was keeping an eye out for thee to come down the track, but when the hour got late I knew ye weren't coming. So why was that? Ye said ye were a man of thy word."

"And that is so. I'm still willing to do the work, but not with such a violent man as Henry Derwin!"

"Why do ye say that?" Jonathan asked, puzzled.

"I was having a quiet jug of ale, when he comes in, grabs me by the throat and accuses me of murdering his children. The man is demon possessed! If it hadn't been for the innkeeper, who knows what would have happened to me!"

"Would ye still come if I keep him away?" asked Jonathan.

"Aye, I said I would. I'll come tonight, but only if ye give me thy word that he won't come near me."

Jonathan made sure he was finished early so that he could get home to warn Henry.

"Hello, Jonathan," Catherine said, opening the door, "we don't often see thee at our door."

"I need to speak to Henry if he's home."

"Don't leave him standing at the door, invite him in woman!" Henry called from the table where he had just started his meal.

"Sorry, Jonathan," she said softly, as she stood to one side.

"Evening, Henry. I've been speaking to Samuel Wright today. I hear you had words at the tavern last night, and it didn't end well."

"Don't speak to me of that man! He makes my blood boil, sitting there denying he's done any wrong! I tell ye, if the innkeeper hadn't stopped me I would have done for him, right there!"

"I thought we agreed that ye wouldn't say anything to him until he did the work?"

"I didn't intend to. I went in for an ale and there he was! My temper took over, especially when he started to deny it."

"Well, I've persuaded him to come and do the work tonight, only I had to give my word that ye would not harm him. What say you, Henry?"

"If he comes here, it will be the last thing he does! Merely *thinking* of the man makes me angry!"

"That may be, and understandably so, but if he doesn't do it, it will cost a tidy sum to get someone else. Let me be here; I'll see to it that he does the work. Take you and thy family next door with Beth, then when it's done it's up to thee."

"Henry, Jonathan has a good plan. Please let him handle it," said Catherine concerned.

"Stay out of it, woman! This is men's business," replied Henry sternly. "So be it, Jonathan. Let him come, but, by God, if I see him ..."

"Ye won't. I'll be back after a hasty bite of food," said Jonathan.

"Jonathan, he's coming! Go and get Henry and his family, quickly, before he knocks on their door," Isabel said, peering out of the shutters.

Jonathan hurried up the track to meet Samuel, giving Henry and his family time to go next door. "Ye decided to come then?"

"So, ye doubted that I would? Is it safe for me to go in?" Samuel asked.

"Aye, he's gone out. It's just the two of us. Would ye like a hand with the timbers?" Jonathan asked.

"Aye, that I would," replied Samuel.

They made their way into the cottage. Samuel looked around the room and remarked, "Looks a homely place. I'll carry on upstairs then."

Jonathan followed with the timbers.

"Down there," Samuel said, pointing to the corner for the timbers.

"Do ye need any help?" Jonathan asked.

"Nay, I'm best left alone. It won't take me long."

I'll be next door but I'll come back in a while to see how ye are getting on."

"Nay need. I'll come down when I'm finished."

With a nod, Jonathan left and returned to his home.

"How long will he be in my house?" asked Henry.

"He won't be long, he says," replied Jonathan.

"The thought of that man in my house makes my blood boil! I don't know how long I can keep myself from going in there to deal with him!" Henry said with a raised voice.

"Please, Henry, not in front of the children," Catherine pleaded.

"I said I'd be back to check on him in a while. Leave it with me, Henry. The work will soon be done, then you can go back and he'll be out of thy life," said Jonathan.

"Samuel Wright will never be out of my life!" Henry said bitterly.

Samuel studied the words scratched on the alcove door. He could make out the first three words: 'Enter and be', but not the last word 'Damedius', written in Latin. Curious, he cut the binding with his knife and opened the door. The room was dark and there was a trace of the smell of smoke in the stale air.

He stepped in to look around, and noticed immediately that the light of his candle reflected on something shiny on the wall. His eyes focused on the little silver cross that was nailed to the middle crossbeam. It occurred to him that, as he was going to board up the room, he could remove the cross and sell it and no one would ever know. He fetched some pincers from his tool bag to prise the nail out, but when he took hold of the cross, blood spurted out from the beam onto to his face and chest, making him drop the cross.

As he stood there in stunned silence, the door behind him slammed shut, blowing his candle out. Panicking, he lunged to open the door but found that it was held fast, which he couldn't understand as the door opened outwards and there couldn't be anything on the other side to stop it. He tried with his shoulder, using all his strength, but found it would not move. He couldn't even use his tools as they were on the other side of the door.

A crackling sound like burning wood made him turn round. On the middle beam, where the cross had been, an ember of fire had started to glow and smoke began to fill the room, making him choke. Gasping for air, he hammered on the door and called for help, but he remembered that he was alone in the house. To his terror, screaming voices started to fill the room, "I'm burning! I'm drowning!" He felt the life draining away from him as he saw the wooden floorboards coming up at him.

As some time had passed, Jonathan went back next door and climbed the stairs to see how Samuel was getting along.

"Are ye there, Samuel?" he called out. There was no answer.

Jonathan could see that the bindings on the door had been cut, and felt sure that Samuel must be in there. He remembered what the priest had said about not entering the room but now he had no choice. Holding his candle high, he slowly opened the door, to see Samuel Wright's body on the floor. The face was so gaunt and colourless, it looked as if the life had been sucked out of him. Jonathan hurriedly left the room, closing the door behind him, and rushed next door.

"Are ye alright, husband?" Isabel said, "Ye look as though ye have seen a ghost!"

"Aye, I'm alright. I need Henry to come with me."

Henry followed Jonathan outside.

"What's the problem?" Henry asked.

"Quick, upstairs! He's dead!" Jonathan said, leading the way.

"What do ye mean, he's dead?"

"He's dead in that room! I think whatever is in there has taken him too. He's gone the way of the children."

Henry opened the door and glanced down at the body. Standing over him with the candle, he said, "Look! He has the same bloody handprint on him as my Tommy and Margaret. He got what he had coming; it saved me the job of doing it!"

"You can't say that Henry! The man's dead," Jonathan said.

"Aye, that might be so, but he cost me two of my children. Good riddance!"

"We'd better send for the priest, Henry. I'll go and get him," Jonathan said, making his way out of the room.

"Nay, wait! If word gets out that he was found dead here, after what I said in the tavern, they will assume I killed him. I won't stand a chance! It will be the hangman's noose at Tyburn for me," Henry said, panicking.

"Don't be daft, man! I know ye didn't kill him. I'll tell them so."

"They know ye are a friend and they'll say ye are only saying that to save me."

"So what do ye want to do? Ye can't leave him here," Jonathan replied.

"Give me a hand to carry him out to his cart. I'll take it to the woods outside the village and bury him, then take the horse and cart back to his home. It will be days before anyone asks after him. They'll think he's sleeping off the drink. No one knows he was coming here, apart from thee. Will ye keep quiet about it, Jonathan?"

"Aye, but what if ye should be seen driving his cart?" asked Jonathan.

"The night is with me and there is a mist. No one will be out on a cold night like this. Now, would ye give me a hand with him?" said Henry.

As they bent down to move him Jonathan noticed something shining. Picking it up he saw that it was a small silver cross.

"He must have tried to use this against whatever it was that killed him."

"The man was too evil for that to do any good! Put it in his pocket. I don't want any trace that he's been here," replied Henry.

The two of them silently carried him out to the back of the cart and covered him with some sacks.

"Henry, the women know he was here and Catherine will ask questions about why he didn't board the door up."

"You're good with the hammer and nails. What say you board up the door while I'm gone, then I'll meet you back here when I'm done burying him."

"If I hadn't been worried about the Squire, I could have had a go at it in the first place. I don't like it, Henry. Something tells me it will go wrong," Jonathan said.

"Nothing will go wrong! Anyway, I have no choice - it's this or the knot at Tyburn."

X1

By the light of the pale moon, Henry found an overgrown area in the woods alongside the track. He climbed down and dragged the body off the cart and into the undergrowth. No sooner had he started to cover it with bracken, he heard the sound of a horse approaching along the track. Panicking, he decided to leave the body as it was and made his way into the dense cover of the woods then headed back to the cottage on foot.

"I was beginning to worry. I thought ye must have been caught, ye have been so long. Did all go well?" Jonathan asked him.

Henry decided not to mention that he'd left the body only half-covered. "Aye, it all went fine. I had better go and fetch Catherine and the children before she starts asking questions."

"Aye, Henry – but we've got a problem! We missed the man's toolbox!"

Henry gasped and closed his eyes, thinking rapidly. "I'll deal with it tomorrow," he said. "We can't do any more tonight."

"Ye have been a long time! We were starting to have concerns that there was trouble with the builder," said Isabel.

"Nay, no trouble. It's all done. We won't be seeing him again," replied Henry. "Let's all go home and get to bed. Thank ye kindly, Jonathan, I shall see thee on the morrow."

Catherine hurried up the stairs with the children. At the sight of the boarded up door she felt she could now relax. As she went to go back downstairs she saw Samuel Wright's toolbox in the corner.

"Henry, the builder has left his toolbox upstairs. Will ye take it with ye tomorrow? I'm sure he will need it."

If only we'd taken it with the body! he thought, angry with himself for missing it. *How can I explain having his toolbox if I take it to the estate?*

"Aye, I'll take it with me," replied Henry.

"It was a long time after Samuel Wright left that ye both came back in here. What were ye doing all that time?" Isabel asked.

"Were ye looking out of the shutters then?"

"I often do when I hear a horse and cart. It was very dark but I could just make out him leaving."

Jonathan was relieved that she assumed it was Samuel. "We were clearing up the mess he left behind."

"That would be the first time Jonathan Earwaker has cleaned up any mess! There's hope yet!" Isabel said laughing.

"Are we going up? I've a long day ahead tomorrow," Jonathan said getting up from his chair.

86

Before Henry harnessed the horse he decided that he would hide the toolbox in his outhouse and cover it up. As no one but the family would go in there, he felt sure it would be safe and he would be at ease about going to work.

The day had been a long, hard one for Jonathan. He was just about to leave for home when he heard the Squire's voice: "Have ye seen Samuel Wright today? I'm sure he didn't turn up this morning. That roof hasn't been touched."

"Nay, Squire, I've not seen him," replied Jonathan.

"Well, if ye come across him, tell him I need to speak to him."

"Aye that I will, Squire."

"I'll not be wanting too many days like that, Isabel. I'm not as young as I used to be!" Jonathan said, sitting down wearily to eat his food.

"Ye will always be young to me, husband! Ye will feel better when ye have eaten and rested," she said smiling at him.

"Have ye heard from next door today?" he said.

"Not really. I saw Catherine when I hung a few things on the line, but we hardly had time to talk. Like thee, I've been busy too."

"Of course ye have, woman," he said with a tinge of sarcasm.

The Squire strode into the coach house to tell Jonathan that he wanted his best carriage made ready for a journey he needed to make. "It's been several days now since that Samuel Wright has been to work. Have ye told him I want to speak to him?"

"Nay, Squire. As I told thee before, I don't know where he is."

"Looks like I'm going to have to make my own enquiries about his whereabouts," the Squire grumbled to himself.

Jonathan pulled up outside the tavern for a quick ale. Making his way over to the bar, he said, "Just the one, Dan."

"In a hurry then, Jonathan?" Dan asked.

"Aye, I'd better not be late getting home tonight - I've been late all week."

"That Squire A'aeth has been in here asking if anyone has seen Samuel Wright. Says he hasn't turned up for work for some days now. He's got it in him to find the man," said Dan.

"Why all the concern about Samuel Wright? I would have thought he was just one more of the workers on the estate," Jonathan remarked.

"Nay, not Samuel. He's not just one of the workers. He told me some time ago: he believed that, if he went the extra mile with his work, the Squire would notice him, see how good a worker he was, and it might secure his job. I suppose the fact that the Squire wants to find him means it paid off for Samuel. Most probably though, he didn't want the trouble of finding someone else. Knowing the Squire's reputation, he *will* find him. You mark my word, he won't rest until he does!" said Dan.

"Well, that will do me," Jonathan said, finishing his ale. "I might call in tomorrow night."

"Aye, I might know a bit more by then," said Dan.

Henry heard a tap on the door and opened it to see Jonathan standing there.

"We need to talk," Jonathan said quietly to him so Catherine wouldn't hear. "The Squire's been asking about Samuel. He's even been asking at the tavern if anyone's seen him. The innkeeper seems to think that he won't give up until he finds him. I thought I should let thee know."

"Thanks, for that, Jonathan," Henry said, looking very concerned.

"I'll be calling at the tavern tomorrow on my way home to see if there's any more talk. I'll keep thee informed. Goodnight then."

"Aye, goodnight to thee," Henry replied.

Father Joel looked up from his sermon notes as Squire A'aeth's man came through the church door.

"Good morrow to thee, Father. Sorry to disturb thee. I work for Squire A'aeth. He sent me to ask thee about Samuel Wright. I take it ye know of him?"

"Aye, I know him. What's he done now?" the priest asked.

"Ye have not heard then? He's been murdered. He was found in the woods. It's likely he was robbed for his tools, but the strange thing is: whoever did it, missed the silver cross he had in his pocket. It's mystifying that he would have such a valuable item on his person and we were wondering if ye can tell us anything, or if ye recognise it?"

"Where's the cross now?" the priest asked.

Taking a mutton cloth out of his pocket, he unwrapped the cross and showed it to the priest.

"Ye say it was in his pocket?"

"Aye, Father. Ye know it?"

"Aye, I do man. The last time I set eyes on it, was when I nailed it to a timber."

"Where would that be then, Father?"

"Henry Derwin's place, on the downs," the priest replied.

"Thank thee, Father. I'll be on my way."

"Are ye not curious as to why I nailed the cross to the timber?" the priest called out to him.

"Nay, Father, I am not. I am paid to find out who murdered Samuel Wright, not who nailed a cross to a timber. By thy leave, Father, I'll say fare thee well."

The priest went back to his study, but found, as hard as he tried, he could not concentrate on the sermon, as his mind was on how the cross could have gone from the alcove room and into Samuel Wright's pocket. He knew that he would have to visit Henry Derwin's place to find out more.

"Father Joel! I wasn't expecting you," Catherine said, trying to tidy her hair and brush down her apron. "Do come in. Pray thee take a seat."

"I'm sorry to come unexpectedly, but I was wondering if I could have another look at the upstairs room?"

"Of course, Father, but there's been no more trouble since we had it boarded up."

"Who boarded it up, and when was it done?" he asked.

"Samuel Wright, the builder. He came the other night. Jonathan, next door, arranged it with him. They both work on Squire A'aeth's estate."

"Do ye know if Samuel Wright went into the room?" Father Joel asked.

"Nay, I do not, Father. We all stayed next door while he did the work."

"I'd like to see the room now if I may?"

The priest headed upstairs, followed by Catherine.

"See, Father Joel – t'is a fine job. We've no need to worry about the children now."

The priest ran his hand over the boarding and said, "Aye, it's a fine job. Did it take him long?"

"Aye, Father. It was late when he went."

"Did ye see him go?"

"Well no, Father Joel. It was Isabel who heard him leaving - she looked out the shutters and saw him drive off on his cart."

The priest frowned, trying to understand how Samuel Wright could have gone into the room, and removed the cross, without any harm coming to him. From his own experience, he knew harm would certainly happen to anybody who entered but, as hard as he tried to unravel the mystery, he couldn't.

"I'll say fare thee well, Catherine. I'll expect to see thee Sunday?"

"Aye, Father, we'll be there."

XII

"Evening, Dan. Just the one."

"In a hurry again, Jonathan?"

"Any more news about Samuel Wright?" Jonathan asked.

"Aye, there is. He's been murdered! A traveller came across his horse and cart in the woods, *and* his body - it was half buried a little way from it. They say that whoever killed him must have been disturbed, as he didn't have time to bury him properly. It must have been for his tools as they weren't on the cart. Those tools were so important - he was never without them. He did some work here at one time and I noticed he'd even carved his initials 'S W' on the box. I tell thee, find those tools and ye find his killer."

Jonathan's mind went back to that night. *A curse on those tools!* He hoped his face wouldn't give anything away.

"I know it's a bit of a shock – ye should see thy face! He was well known around here. I've already had Squire A'aeth's men in here asking questions."

"What sort of questions?" asked Jonathan.

"When was the last time I saw him? Who else was here who might have seen him? Was there any trouble? 'Trouble!' I says. 'This is a tavern. There's always trouble'. But *with* Samuel Wright they asks. 'Aye, I says, there was when Henry Derwin comes in – turning over the table and grabbing him by the throat, calling him a child murderer'. I says I stopped them and told Derwin to go home - I've had too many stools broken. They asked me if he did go, and I said: 'Yes, but as he went out the door he turned to Samuel and said he was going to see he got what was coming to him'."

"What happened next?" Jonathan asked.

"They asked where they could find the man, Derwin. I told them: in one of the cottages up on the downs. Don't he live next door to thee?"

There was a pause before he answered. "Aye, but they have the wrong man. He's not a killer. Ye ought to be careful what ye say, Dan. That talk could cause a lot of harm to a man, especially if he's not guilty."

"I only told what I saw, and it's the truth about Derwin threatening him. Although ye would never expect Henry Derwin to have a temper! I suppose grief over a child can make thee do all sorts of things."

"I tell thee, he didn't do it, Dan."

"Ye seem pretty sure."

"I live next door to him and I wouldn't live next door to a murder."

"Well the Squire's men are on their way there now."

"I'd better make haste! He might need my help," Jonathan said, hurrying to the door.

"I wouldn't get involved, Jonathan!" Dan called after him.

"Ma, there's four men coming down the track!" Isabel's eldest lad called up the stairs.

As she hurried down, there was a knock at the door.

"We are here to see Henry Derwin," a big, swarthy man announced to her.

Isabel stepped back, for the sight of four armed men at the door made her too scared to speak.

"*Henry Derwin*. Is he here?" the man demanded.

"Ye have come to the wrong place. He lives next door, but I don't know if he is home yet."

They said no more, but went round the back and hammered on the Derwin's door. Isabel and her eldest lad followed them and stood outside watching the men enter the cottage, even before there was time for anyone to answer the door.

"Henry Derwin! We're arresting you for the murder of Samuel Wright!"

Before Henry had a chance to answer, his wrists were clapped in irons.

"Search the place, inside and out!" the big man ordered two of his men.

"I don't know any 'Samuel Wright', Henry protested, struggling with the man who held him.

One of the men soon returned; "I've found the tool box! It was hidden in the outhouse." On the lid, for everyone to see, were the carved letters: '$\mathcal{S}$ $\mathcal{W}$'.

"Take him away. We have the proof we need for a hanging!"

Henry turned to Catherine and pleaded, "I didn't kill him! Ye have to believe me!"

Isabel quickly went over to Catherine as Henry was marched away.

"I don't understand, Isabel! They say he killed Samuel Wright. Please tell me he didn't!"

"Of course he didn't," Isabel said, trying not to show her misgivings, having heard Henry speak ill of Samuel.

"What will I do Isabel, what will I do?" she wept.

X111

"Oh Jonathan, I wish ye had been here! It's been terrible; they came and took Henry away for the murder of Samuel Wright. Catherine's in a bad way; she's not stopped crying. They found Samuel Wright's tools in Henry's outhouse. The man in charge said that's all the proof needed for a hanging! I don't understand - how did they get there?" Isabel said anxiously.

"I don't know, Isabel, I don't know." *How stupid could he be to hide them so close to home?* His words that night came back to him: *'I don't like it, something tells me that it will go wrong.'*

"Jonathan, is there anything we can do for Henry?"

"Nay, Isabel. Nothing."

"Can I ask something?" she said, looking worried.

"Ask away, Isabel."

"The other night when Henry's family were in here, I sensed that what ye said about clearing up the mess wasn't true. What was the real reason?" she asked.

"I told thee we were cleaning up his mess. Keep out of it, woman! Don't ever question what I say again. Ye need to busy thyself like other women, cooking and bearing children!" he said angrily.

Isabel knew she had crossed the line with her husband and stayed quiet while he got out his pipe and sat in front of the fire, looking deeply troubled.

"Evening, Jonathan. It's been a few weeks since I've seen thee," said the innkeeper.

"Aye, Dan, it has been. I need a jug tonight! T'is a sad day."

"I take it ye have heard then? They hanged Henry Derwin today at Tyburn."

"Aye, they hanged an innocent man," Jonathan replied.

"Ye are the only one who believed he was innocent," said Dan.

"That's because he was."

"I hear he kept saying he didn't do it when he was in Newgate, and even right up to the time they tied the knot round his neck. How's his wife and family holding up?" Dan asked.

"I don't know; I haven't been home yet. I'm not looking forward to it either."

"What will happen to them now? I suppose they'll have to move out as the cottage is only for those who work for the Squire, and Derwin ain't going to be working for him again!" Dan chuckled.

Jonathan banged his tankard down hard and left the tavern.

"Something I said?" Dan called to him as he went out the door.

"Pray sit down, husband, and eat thy food," Isabel said.

"How's she coping next door? I take it ye have been in there?"

"Aye, I've tried my best to comfort her; she's totally at a loss about what to do. She keeps asking me, but I'm as much at a loss as she is. What will happen to her Jonathan?"

The owner at the Black Dog thinks she will have to leave as the cottages are for estate workers, and now Henry has gone . . . I reckon it won't be long before the Squire's man will be at her door, making sure she's moved out," he replied.

"Couldn't they move in here?"

"Don't be daft, woman! We have no room, and can just about put food on the table for *us*. Even if I wanted them to, I doubt if the Squire would allow it."

Isabel kept quiet after that as she noticed that, every time she mentioned anything about next door, he would get angry. It was puzzling, as he and Henry had become friends.

After Jonathan had left for work and the children were up and fed, she went next door to see how Catherine was.

"Come in, Isabel. I'm so pleased ye have come. I needed someone to talk to."

"I thought ye might. Where will ye go now Catherine?" Beth asked.

"We'll go back to Devon, to stay with my folks."

"Oh, I thought ye came from around here."

"No, Henry's family are from this area. I couldn't stay here, even if I wanted; there's too much talk about me being the wife of a murderer. Besides, I know the terms of living here - that the Squire will want me out now Henry's gone. I'll be packing up today and loading the cart tomorrow morning."

"Oh, Catherine, I shall miss thee. Ye have been a good friend."

"Likewise, Isabel," she said, hugging her.

"I've made something for thee," Isabel said, handing her a small package, wrapped in a scrap of cloth.

Catherine unwrapped it and smiled. "Oh, Isabel, it's a friendship band! What does this message on the cloth say?"

"It says:

> *'To my best friend, Catherine,*
> *lest we forget each other.*
> *May our friendship go on forever.'*
> *Isabella.'*

"They're such lovely words and fine embroidery! Where did ye learn to read and write such words?"

"My father was a teacher. I'm glad ye like it," Isabel said.

"I will always wear it and treasure it," Catherine replied.

"I'll send young Henry round in the morning to help ye load up, he's a strong lad," Isabel said.

"Thanks, Isabel, I'd better make a start. There's so much to do."

"I shall see thee on the morrow," Isabel said, leaving sadly.

"Ma! Henry next door is fighting with our Alfred and Mrs Earwaker is trying to stop them!"

Catherine rushed outside. "Stop that now, Alfred! Get inside with thee!"

"But he started it, Ma! He called Pa 'a murderer'! I'm glad we're moving away from them. They're always in our house," Alfred protested loudly.

He went in, leaving his mother outside talking to Isabel. On one of the shelves he saw the gift that Isabel had given her. With Henry's words about his father still ringing in his mind, he snatched the gift angrily and went up to his room. He had found a hiding place that none of his family knew about. He removed the loose wooden dowel from a hole in the beam to reveal an ideal hiding place for small things. He rolled the gift back up in the cloth and poked it in the hole, pushed the dowel back in and went back downstairs.

"I could hear the shouting outside!" Isabel said.

"Sorry, Isabel! The lad didn't mean what he said; he's upset."

"Don't worry about that, Catherine. It's understandable – that was a terrible thing for Henry to say!" She turned to her son, "Ye must apologise to Alfred, Henry. Now get back to loading before I tell thy Pa that ye have been fighting! "

Isabel went back indoors, trying to calm her anger. It wasn't long before she could hear a man's voice outside. Looking out of the shutters, she recognised the same big man who had come the other day to take Henry away. He had been sent by the Squire to make sure Catherine was out of the cottage.

Isabel had busied herself putting together some food for their long journey. "Will ye be alright?" she said, as she handed the basket to Catherine.

"Aye, Isabel, we will. We had better get going; t'is a long journey and we'll need to make it there before dark."

"Catherine, ye are not wearing the band I made thee!"

"I was hoping ye wouldn't notice. I put it down last night and I cannot find it anywhere. I asked the children but they've not seen it. I'm so sorry, but I promise I'll never forget thee. Fare thee well, Isabel," Catherine said with tears in her eyes.

"Fare thee well, Catherine. God go with thee."

The Squire's man closed and locked the cottage door, nodded his head at Isobel and said "Good morrow to thee, ma'm," and made his way off.

"Did they get away all right?" Jonathan asked.

"Aye, t'was a sad parting. I shall miss her. But t'is better they've gone - who knows what might have happened to them if they'd stayed. Who do ye think will be next door now?"

"That I cannot say, Isabel, but methinks it will be a long time before anyone comes to live there. Rumour has it the place has a curse on it."

PART 11

14

Cathy came through the front door to hear the phone ringing. "Hello," she answered, slightly out of breath.

"Mrs Dawson? John Miles here, from Harbourne's. We have a place that's just come on our books, which I think meets your requirements. I was wondering if you and your husband would like to arrange a viewing today?"

"Oh, okay. Can you tell me a little more about it before I ring my husband?" she asked.

"It's a large period cottage, a little further out than you wanted, but it has the land you requested."

"It sounds great, but I'm not sure if my husband can get away from the office today. Can I ring you back?"

"Of course, Mrs Dawson. I would just say though, properties like this don't often come on the market. You're my first port of call and, without being too pushy, I don't expect it to be on our books very long."

"Thank you, Mr Miles. I'll come back to you as soon as I can."

"I got your message. What's up? Are you missing me?"

"Oh yes, dear. The agent's phoned; they've got something for us to view. It sounds as though it's the sort of thing we're looking for, George. Can you get away early today so we can view it?"

"I'll get Sandra to reschedule things. Ask him to email me the address over and we'll meet him there at four. I'll be home about 3; be ready to go."

"Love you," she said excitedly.

"Love you too."

Cathy heard the car pull up and hurried to the front door, briefly checking her appearance in the hall mirror.

"Do you know where it is? she asked.

"Yes, it's near a village called 'Cornwood' on the downs, about 45 minutes from here."

"Can't wait to see it; it's exciting!" Cathy said, buckling her seat belt. It was quite a pleasant journey and the time passed quickly.

"*Turn left*," the sat nav instructed. They made their way down a long drive. "*You have arrived at your destination*," came the voice again. As they pulled up they could see the agent waiting for them.

"Good afternoon Mr & Mrs Dawson. John Miles," he said, shaking their hands. "You obviously found it all right. My sat nav kept losing its signal; it must be the area."

"Yes, no problem. It brought us straight here," replied George.

"Well, here it is. What do you think? Before we go inside, I have to tell you that it does need modernising. I know you said you didn't want anything that had to have a lot of work done, but at least that way you can put your own stamp on it," the agent said, leading the way to the front door.

The door creaked as it opened, revealing a large room with a host of oak wall and ceiling beams, and a large inglenook fireplace with an old iron cooking range.

"It has five bedrooms, two bathrooms, a large lounge, a kitchen and this room. I suppose you could call it a 'family room', or make it whatever you'd like. There are several outer buildings. It stands on two acres of land. Would you like to have a look around?"

"Lead the way," George said as Cathy smiled and nodded.

They went through to the lounge, which was larger than the family room, again with plenty of dark oak beams and another large fireplace.

"It's quite dark in here - not much light from those little windows," remarked George.

"I love the cosiness of it, George. It has so much character!" Cathy said.

"These old period places *were* dark; the lead light windows didn't help, but that's how they were built back then," replied the agent.

"How old is the place?" asked George.

"About five hundred years; Grade 2 Listed," the agent replied.

"By the look and feel of the place, I'd guess no one has lived here for years," remarked George.

"I believe it's been empty for about five years. An elderly lady lived here and then passed away. Apparently there was some legal dispute with the family, and it's taken all this time to sort it out so that it can be sold," responded the agent.

"How long did she live here, then?" asked Cathy.

"I don't know too much about the history of the place but, as you can see, I don't think it's been touched since the forties. Apparently, she didn't like change, and was a bit of a recluse. I should think the parish church would have records about how long she lived here. Well, that's the downstairs. Would you like to see upstairs?"

"Lead the way," George said with a hint of disappointment in his voice.

They made their way up the old, winding, wooden staircase, to the first floor landing.

Cathy was surprised to see a second staircase leading to another floor, "There are more rooms up there?"

"Yes, three on this floor and two attic rooms. This is the main bedroom," the agent said, showing them in. "As you can see it's a large double room and there's a bathroom next door. With a bit of work, I'm sure you could incorporate an en-suite into the room. Let me show you the other bedrooms. This next room is the second largest, but still a double."

"Smells musty in here. With the amount of dust laying around and the old forties' style wallpaper, I should think no one's used it for *many* years, let alone five," said George.

"Well, I did say the old lady didn't like change," remarked the agent.

"You can say that again," said George, ruefully.

"This is the last bedroom; the smallest, but still plenty of room. I think this one must have been added over the years but I'm not sure when. Well that leaves the upper rooms, if you'd like to follow me."

They followed the agent up the steep, newish staircase to the attic. "Mind your head, the doors are very low," the agent said. Up here are the two attic rooms; as you can see one leads into the other, separated by the wide chimneybreast."

"People slept up here?" asked Cathy.

"Probably children - they had large families when these places were built; they made use of the space," replied the agent.

"How did they get up here? That staircase looks recent," Cathy remarked.

"Ladder," he said.

"You said there were two bathrooms?" asked George.

"Yes, if we make our way down, there's one here," he said showing them, "With a nice original forties' style bath, and the other one is on the ground floor, which I'll show you on the way out,"

"It's very small, not what you could call a bathroom," remarked George.

"Probably the old lady had it put in so she didn't have to climb the stairs, but I'm sure it could be turned into just a downstairs toilet. Well, what do think of it? asked the agent.

"We did want a place that required no work, and I can see this place needing a huge amount of, not only work, but money," George said putting his finger on a crack in the wall.

"I'm pretty sure, Mr Dawson, when it's finished it would be worth several times more than the asking price, and I'm sure the price can be negotiated."

"Can we see outside?" George asked.

"Of course," the agent said and led them round the back of the house. "As you can see there are many outer buildings, some look sound and others need a little work."

George walked off with the agent, leaving Cathy looking around the outer buildings.

"How much land is with the property?"

"Two acres - made up from a small orchard, vegetable garden, and a copse."

"How far does the copse go back?" George said.

"It has quite a depth; I should imagine it would supply all the wood you would need for the fire."

George looked around for Cathy, but couldn't see her, "She's always doing this, wandering off," he said.

"My wife's the same," the agent said, chuckling.

"Cathy!" he called out.

Cathy came out from one of the buildings. "I could have a wonderful studio in there," she said walking over to them, "and come and see what else I've found!"

They followed her over to a small circular wall covered in ivy. "It's an old well," she said looking down it.

"I didn't know about that," the agent said.

"Can you see water down there?" George asked her.

"I don't know; it's too dark to see, but I have a way of finding out," she said taking a stone and dropping into the well.

There was a brief silence, then a splash.

"There's your answer, George," Cathy said.

"Don't tell me that's the only source of water to the house! I suppose there is mains water here?"

"Good heavens, Mr Dawson, of course there's mains water, as there is electricity."

"I had to ask; it's like living in the past here," George said. He turned back to face the house. "The thatch looks the worse for wear. I shouldn't think there's much life left in it, and I'd bet the insurance on the place would be steep."

Before the agent could answer, Cathy said, "It looks like long straw, and if it is, the life span is between 15 and 25 years, and nowadays you can have it coated with a fire retardant. Providing the chimney is swept every year, there shouldn't be a problem."

"That's no time at all! I wouldn't want to have the roof re-thatched (and a pricey sum it would be), to have it lasting that short a time," George said.

109

"Well, we could always have it thatched with Norfolk reed, which has a life span of 50 to 60 years," Cathy replied.

"You seem to know an awful lot about thatching, Mrs. Dawson," the agent said.

"That's because delving into the history of old cottages is a hobby of mine. I've always wanted to live in one; they have so much to tell, with all that's taken place in them over the centuries. And somehow I think this place has an interesting story, yet to revealed," she replied.

"I imagine it has, Mrs Dawson."

They were about to return to the front of the building, when Cathy stopped and went over to the wall of the house. "Was this previously *two* cottages?"

"I'm not sure. Why do you ask?" the agent said.

"There are signs that there was once a door here. See how the brickwork has been altered?" she said pointing to a vertical line in the wall.

"I see what you mean," her husband said, "I didn't realise you knew so much about old buildings."

"Going to night school with Izzy, and studying the history of buildings helped. There's a lot of things you don't know about me, dear," she replied with a smile. "And if there *were* originally two dwellings, they were probably tied cottages for workers and it's likely that those tiny windows didn't even have glass in them – just shutters."

The agent interrupted them, "Shall we make our way round to the front?"

As they stood by the car, taking a final look at the building, the agent asked, "What do you think of the property? Do you think you could do something with it?"

"Well, Mr Miles, I can see the potential of the place but I'm not sure if we're prepared to undertake the amount of work required. We'll give it some thought and let you know," George said.

"As I said to Mrs Dawson, properties like this don't hang around for long. I wouldn't leave it too long making your mind up."

On the way back, Cathy said, "You know I like the place, George. I think, after we've finished doing it up, it'll look like one of those pictures on a box of chocolates, really charming and picturesque."

"Yes, I guessed you liked the place, but it needs so much done to it. It hasn't been lived in for years. Let's keep looking, Cathy; I'm sure we'll find what we're looking for - a place that's more up together."

Cathy knew George wasn't too keen on the place and that, for her to have her way, she would have to work her special charm on him.

"Good day at the office?" she said as he sat down to unwind with a glass of wine. Snuggling up to him on the sofa, she said, "George Henry, you know you love me and how much I love you, and you know how you like to do nice things for me?"

"Yes, … the only time you call me by both names is when you want me to buy you something. What is it this time?" he replied, thinking that it was probably a new dress or a holiday.

She said, "Will you buy that cottage for me? I can't stop thinking about it! I can't explain it, but it's as if it's drawing me to it."

"It's not the money, Cathy. I know we can afford it, but it's the amount of work. I know you! You will take it on yourself, and I don't want you wearing yourself out."

"But you know how I love old buildings, and to own one would make a dream come true! I'd only be doing the decorating and minor alterations. We'd obviously get professionals for the plumbing, thatching and electrical work. It would give me something to do while you are at work."

"Cathy, it's still a lot of work. Do we really want a place with five bedrooms?"

"We'd only have three spare, and I'm sure we can fill them over time," she said.

"How do you make that out then? We will have one, and one from five leaves four."

"Our baby will need one," she said softly, not knowing what his reaction would be.

"And then there's all the land outside to be looked after. Wait a minute, did you say: *baby?*"

"I didn't say anything because I wanted to be sure before telling you, but yes, *we're going to have a baby*, George! And before you say anything, I know that I can get the place finished in time."

"That's not what I was going to say, Cathy. That's the most wonderful news I could ever wish for! Say it again, sweetheart!"

"What, that I could get the place finished in time?" she said, teasing him.

"No! You know what I mean; say it again."

"We're going to *have a baby!*" she repeated ecstatically.

"What a gift you have given me!" he said as he pulled her into his arms and kissed her. "I suppose I'm going to have to buy you that cottage now as a thank you present?"

"Thank you! Thank you!" she said, smiling to herself, now that she'd finally got what she wanted.

"You've got to promise me, Cathy, that you will *not* overdo it, especially now that you're going to have our baby."

"I promise you, George, I won't; I can get Izzy to help me.   So, can I tell the agent we want it?" she said excitedly.

"Yes, give him a ring …"

15

"Izzy, I've got some great news! You know that cottage I was telling you about that George and I went to see the other day, the place I loved and he didn't? Well, George bought it for me!" Cathy squealed into phone.

"How did you manage that? You said he was adamant that it needed too much work," replied Izzy.

"I had a little something up my sleeve! I knew when he heard it he wouldn't be able to say 'no' to me."

"And what was that? Is there something you haven't told me? Your *best friend?*" Izzy said.

"I told him I was pregnant."

"You told him *what?* That's a mean thing to say, Cathy, just to get your own way."

"It's true."

"How could you keep something like that from your closest friend?"

"I've only just found out myself, and George had to be the first to know, Izzy, being my *husband!*"

"Sorry, Cathy, of course. I bet he was over the moon!"

"He was excited, but insisted he didn't want me to overwork myself, doing up the cottage. Which brings me to something I wanted to ask you."

"Yes..."

"Will you come and help me? It would be so much fun doing it together?"

"How did I know that was coming, Cathy?"

"That's what becomes of being *best friends* and knowing me so well, Izzy!"

"I'll say one thing for you, Cathy. You're a natural at getting what want - you know all the right things to say," Izzy replied, drily.

"So I take it it's a 'yes'."

"When do we start?"

"We'll go and have a look at it tomorrow. I can't wait to show it to you!"

"Well, what do you think of it, Izzy?" Cathy said, as they pulled up outside.

"It's beautiful," Izzy replied.

"Come on, let's go in. I can't wait to show you the rooms!" Cathy said, opening the door.

Brimming with curiosity, Izzy followed Cathy through the door.

"This is the kitchen-come-living-room; I suppose it'll be used the most. And over here is a bathroom, although I'm going to take out the bath and make it a downstairs cloakroom. What do you think about all the wonderful beams?" Cathy asked.

Izzy didn't answer. Cathy noticed that she was just staring around the room.

"Izzy, are you alright? You didn't answer."

"Sorry Cathy, I had one of those 'déja vu' feelings, when I came in. That was weird. You were saying?"

"I was just asking what you thought of the beams?"

"They're great. It's like going back in time. When was the last time anybody lived here?"

"The agent said about five years ago, but the place hasn't really been touched since the 1940s." Showing Izzy the other room, she said, "This is the main room. Don't you love the fireplace? Wait till you see the staircase! Mind your head as we go up."

"I love the rickety-rackety floor levels," Izzy said.

"Yes, I think that's what gives it character. This is going to be the main bedroom; fair size, isn't it?" Cathy said. She could see that Izzy wasn't responding to her enthusiasm.

"This is weird, Cathy. I have the same strange feeling in this room as downstairs. How many rooms up here?"

"Two more on this floor and two upstairs in the attic, plus a bathroom. If you think this looks as if it hasn't been touched, you wait till you see upstairs. Come next door and see what will be the nursery before we go up. I'll be able to hear the baby cry even without one of those monitors." Cathy went out, thinking Izzy was behind her. "This little room has apparently been added over the years but I'm not sure how long ago. Mind you, by the time I've finished researching the place, I *will* know," Cathy said.

"Sorry, Cathy, I was still in the other room. What were you saying?"

Cathy smiled and said, "Never mind, let's go up to the attic." She led the way enthusiastically.

"Who would live up here? It could only be midgets or children. The doors are so low you really have to mind your head," said Izzy.

"I know, but it's all original since the day it was built. What would you say, Izzy, 1500s?"

"By the construction of the beams, I think I'd agree with you," she nodded.

116

"I so love it, don't you?" Cathy said.

"So when do we start?" Izzy asked.

"Well, the roof has to be re-thatched first, and then there's the rewiring and plumbing. When that's done we can start decorating, but meanwhile we can have fun choosing the colour schemes for the rooms. Let me quickly show you outside then we'll have to get back."

"Is that the time? I'll have to be back by five, Cathy. You know what John's like if he gets home and there's not a meal on the table!"

On the way back, Cathy asked Izzy which room was her favourite.

"The first one; the kitchen-come-living-room, and the room above. To me there was a homely atmosphere."

"What about the room I'm going to make into a nursery? Do you think it's too big? Or do you think I should make the smaller room the baby's room?" Cathy asked.

"Don't know, Cathy. The smaller room is a little too far from your room to hear the baby, but if you're going to use a monitor then I would use that one."

"Didn't you like the other room then?" Cathy asked.

"There was something about it. That was the reason I was such a long time in there."

"Like what?"

"I sensed something in there. To me, it wasn't a happy room," Izzy replied.

"You were always funny like that, 'sensing' things, Izzy."

"Well, when you consider the age of the building, a lot of people must have lived there and, I dare say, died too. Do you remember, we discussed at night school whether buildings can retain an atmosphere from tragic events?"

117

"Well, if that *is* true, I'm going to fill the place with happiness and love, so people in years to come will sense it!" Cathy replied. "Well, I've got you back on time to get John's meal ready. I'll give you a call tomorrow."

"Okay," Izzy replied reaching over to hug her.

"Hi Izzy, I couldn't stop thinking about what you said yesterday about all the people that must have lived at the cottage over the years. I was wondering if you'd like to come with me to the parish church in the area, to see if they'd have records that would give us some information?"

"What time are you picking me up?"

"You didn't need much persuasion!"

"You know me, Cathy. I love this sort of stuff."

Pulling up outside the church, Cathy said, "By the looks of this place I would say it's about the same period. I was hoping it would be. What do you reckon?"

Izzy pursed her lips and nodded.

They made their way up the gravelled path, only to find the oak doors locked.

"That's a shame! Maybe it's only opened at the weekends," Cathy said.

"Well, while we're here, let's have a look at the old gravestones. Some of them must be hundreds of years old," Izzy said.

"Come and see this stone, Izzy! I know you like old English names; you'll find this one interesting."

Izzy didn't answer. Cathy could see her looking down at a stone, absorbed. She went over to join her.

"I can't make out all the writing; it has weathered so much, but I think the name is Isabella something waker." Izzy said.

Clearing some of the moss from the stone, Cathy frowned and said, "I can make out an 'E' and something, something, but the dates are still quite clear: '1484 to 1530'. 'Bel, wife of Jonathan something E------r'."

"She must have been someone special to have a stone in those days, and, whoever she was, her husband must have loved her. 'Beloved wife of Jonathan ---waker'. I wonder what her story was." A shiver went down her spine.

"Don't know, Izzy, maybe a story of love. You alright? You're not cold are you?"

"No, I just had a feeling of someone walking over my grave." To lighten the mood, she said, "You're such a romantic, Cathy!"

"Can I help you?" The voice from behind them made them jump. Turning round they saw it belonged to a grey-haired man in a black frock and white collar.

"You made us jump!" Cathy wasn't sure how to address him. She tentatively added, "Father?" When he didn't correct her, she assumed she was right. "I'm Cathy Dawson and this is my friend, Izzy Earnshaw. My husband and I have just bought the old cottage on the downs, and we were hoping to find out a bit of its history, such as who lived there over the years. Are we right in thinking that the parish church would hold such records?"

"Nice to meet you, Cathy and Izzy. I'm Father Michael. Yes, Miriam Myrtle's old place. I did hear that it had been bought by some 'city folk', after standing empty so long."

"Actually, my ancestors (on my father's side) are from somewhere around here."

"What name would that be, then?" asked Father Michael.

"Derwin."

"I didn't know that," Izzy said, frowning.

119

"Ah, yes a good old local name," Father Michael nodded.

"Do you know it then, Father?" asked Cathy.

"Yes, I have come across the name over the years."

"No, the cottage!" she said.

"Yes, of course, the cottage. I made a few house calls there when Miriam wasn't able to get around anymore. She had always been a bit of a recluse and it's a big place to be on your own. If she'd slipped on those stairs nobody would have known – as I told her many times on my visits. She would always reply, "I'm not on my own, I hear them speaking to me." When I asked her *who* was speaking to her, she would reply: "It's the voices, the voices! Up there!" she would say, pointing to the ceiling. I couldn't get any sense out of her. It wasn't long after that I found her lying at the foot of the stairs .... I'm sorry - I got a bit carried away there. I think we have some old records in the archives, but they were a bit hit and miss in those days. Let's go and see if we can find them and blow some of the dust off; that's if you have time?"

Cathy looked at Izzy, knowing she had to be back before five. "What do you think?"

"Let's do it! We've come all this way; I'm sure it shouldn't take too long," Izzy responded eagerly.

They followed Father Michael to a side door into the church, and through to the vestry.

"What a wonderful sense of peace in here," Izzy said to Father Michael.

"Yes, I must confess you do get used to it, living here," he replied.

"You live in the church?" Izzy asked.

"Sort of, my little place is attached to the back of the building."

"Is the church still used for services?" Izzy asked.

"Only on special occasions: Christmas, Easter and Harvest Festival times. Apart from that, we don't see anyone here. Ah! This is what I've been looking for. I knew it was buried here somewhere," he said, opening an old wooden chest. He took out an ancient-looking book and placed it on the table. "So, how far do you want to go back?"

"From when the cottage was built, I suppose; if it goes back that far," Cathy said, hopefully.

Well, I suppose that would be somewhere near the beginning, as the cottages are round about the same age as when the church records began. Here you are, first entry:

'Squire A'aeth, to him was a child born, Alfred William A'aeth 1513.'

Yes, he went on to have several children. It's well known that he was the owner of a large estate in this area. He would have owned many tied cottages around here, including the cottage that you've bought, I should think. Now let's see what other entries there are. He ran his finger along the 'Deaths' column and read out a few names:

'William Sykes, Shopkeeper. Samuel Wright, Builder. Daniel Green, Innkeeper.'

"Does it list the tenants of the tied cottages on the estate?" Izzy asked, trying to speed things up.

"I think that might be listed under a different section. Ah! I think this is what you might be looking for," he said and started to read aloud:

'Two cottages, erected by Samuel Wright, Builder, on the downs. Cottage one: occupied on the 12ᵗʰ day January in the year of our Lord 1513 by a Jonathan Earwaker, occupation: Cartwright, his wife Isabella and twelve children.'

"Earwaker! Cathy, that's what it said on the stone. Sorry, Father, we were trying to decipher it when you found us. A part of the name was missing and we couldn't work out what the missing letters were. Isabella Earwaker is buried here in the churchyard. That's a bit unusual, isn't it, Father, for a common person to have a headstone? I mean, her husband was only a wheelwright."

"Yes, you're right - but who knows the story behind it? Maybe her parents were of money. Yes, there's an entry of her death: 'died giving birth'. It was quite common in those days. It says here, they lived at the cottage for seventeen years. I assume when the wife died, Jonathan moved away. There is another entry here:

'13ᵗʰ Day January in the year of our Lord 1513: Cottage two occupied by Henry George Derwin, gardener, his wife Catherine and ten children'."

"I bet you're related to them, Cathy!" said Izzy. "Sorry, Father."

He continued: "Ah I see here, he lost two of his children, a 'Tomas Giles' aged three and 'Margaret Louise' aged five'."

"What about Henry Derwin and his wife? What happened to them?" Cathy asked.

"Ah! This looks interesting. Somewhere in the church graveyard would be Tommy and Margaret's graves. You would never find them as they would have only been marked by a simple wooden cross, that's if they were marked at all. But it says here:

Henry Gerge Derwin was hanged for the murder of Samuel Wright at Tyburn on the 13th day of June in the year of our Lord 1513.

His wife and children would have been evicted from the cottage. That surprises me; I would have thought something like that would have been kept quiet and not been entered, but there it is," the priest said.

"Poor woman, having lost two of her children and then her husband; that's sad. Does it say which cottage she lived in?" Izzy asked.

"Not really; only that the cottages were numbered as 'one' and 'two'." Reading down a little further, he said, "No! I stand corrected: 'Jonathan Earwaker – one' and 'Henry Derwin – two'."

"Does it say who moved in to cottage No. 2 after the family moved out?" Cathy asked.

Father Michael spent a little time looking down the section on the tied cottages. "That's strange; either no one kept the records updated or nobody lived there till 1540. That's a long time! There would have to have been a very good reason for it to stay empty for that long," he said, turning the page over, hoping to find some more information.

"Would Samuel Wright, be buried here?" Cathy asked.

"I'm not sure. There are a few old gravestones still standing, but I'm sure he wouldn't have had a stone. Let's see who else lived there," he said.

Izzy nudged Cathy and pointed at her watch. I'm sorry, Father Michael, but we've run out of time. Can we come back another day?"

"Certainly! I'm here late mornings, most days. I'll look forward to seeing you again, now you're a part of the parish, so to speak."

"Actually, Father, I'll let Izzy come back. I want to get on with renovating the cottage – there's so much to do and I haven't got long," she said, patting her tummy.
Thank you for your time, Father."

"You're welcome. I've quite enjoyed myself, delving into the archives," he replied cheerfully.

Father Michael watched them drive off and went back into the vestry to tidy up the boxes. He put the record book back in its box, and was about to put it into the trunk when he noticed what appeared to be another book wrapped in an old cloth. He untied the cord and unwrapped it. It was indeed an old book, bound in leather and he was surprised at how heavy it was. He opened it to see written: 'Father Joel, 1513', and he could see it contained his daily writings. As he turned the pages, his eyes caught a heading and the name: 'Henry George Derwin'. His attention was riveted to the entry and he quickly started reading.

'13ᵗʰ Day of February in the year of our Lord, 1513, Henry George Derwin reported the death of his son, Tomas Giles Derwin, age three'. It went on to say: 'There was a great atmosphere of sorrow at the home when I paid a visit.'

'On the 13ᵗʰ Day of March in the year of our Lord, 1513, Henry George Derwin reported the death of his daughter, Margaret Louise Derwin, age five. It is unusual for a family to have so much adversity in such a short space of time.'

'12th Day of April in the year of our Lord, 1513: Visited Pike's salvage yard. It appears that the evil in the Derwin cottage had originated from a curse out of the pit of hell, that has somehow attached itself to an oak beam due to the practice of the dark arts by a certain Tobias Spry. If Pike's tale is true, then Tobias Spry invoked a curse on Daniel Derwin and his descendants. Even though I fear what I have to do on the morrow, I know that it has to be done. May the Lord protect me.'

13th Day of April in the year of our Lord, 1513: Performed exorcism at the cottage of Henry Derwin. Greater evil than I have ever known was there. I am troubled of mind as to whether the dark forces and the curse of Tobias Spry have been laid to rest. Only time will tell.

13th Day of May in the year of our Lord, 1513: Squire A'aeth's men called inquiring about a silver cross found on Samuels Wright's body. I am of great discomfit as to how the cross came to be in the hands of Samuel Wright, since I nailed it to the cursed beam in Derwin's cottage. A heavy burden lies within my soul that the evil spirit in the room is not at rest. But, by the grace of God, the door to the room has been boarded up, which is now the only containment of the evil spirit that lies within. God help anyone living in such a place if the boarding were to be removed, for who could stand such evil that would be unleashed?

13th Day of June in the year of our Lord, 1513: Henry George Derwin hanged at Tyburn for the murder of Samuel Wright.

Father Michael turned the page to see if any more entries had been made, but there were none. He began to feel deeply concerned for Cathy Dawson and her husband, soon to be living in the cottage. Thinking back to his visits to Miriam Myrtle at the old place, he remembered her claims about hearing voices upstairs, and how he'd dismissed them as the ramblings of an old lady. Now, however, if what Father Joel had written was true, and he had no reason to doubt it, it would explain a lot. He knew what he had to do, but how could he gain access to the house without telling them everything? After all, they might not even believe in dark forces. The last thing he wanted to do was to scare them, but until whatever was in that house had been put to rest, Cathy Dawson and her husband were in danger. He decided to talk to Izzy next time she came. After all, the Dawsons wouldn't be moving in until the place was finished.

16

George sat down on the sofa. "How's my project manager been today, not overworking? I hope you've been looking after our baby?" he said as Cathy handed him his usual glass of wine.

"No, husband, I'm not overworking. I haven't been to the cottage today; in fact I've had a day off and, yes, I *am* looking after our baby. I met up with Izzy and we went to the old parish church near the cottage to find out a bit of the history of the place."

"I'll bet you enjoyed that. Find out anything interesting?"

"Yes, I was right about it originally being two cottages. They were built in 1513, and apparently a man who lived in one of them was hanged for murder! Oh, no the phone," she said, "If that's work for you, I'm going to tell them you're busy."

"It won't be; I'm not expecting any calls. It's probably for you," he said.

"Hi Cathy, I couldn't wait till tomorrow to tell you. I remembered what you said about your ancestors coming from around that area, so I couldn't help looking on one of those ancestry sites. I put in your details and traced all the way back to the Middle Ages. Guess what? You are related to Henry Derwin! In fact, you are a *direct descendant*! I've also been looking at the notes I made at the church. Did you realise that the women who lived there, Catherine and Isabella, have the same names as us?" Izzy said excitedly.

"Well, I'm blowed, after all the years I've known you, I didn't know that 'Izzy' is short for 'Isabella'," Cathy replied.

"Apparently it's a very old Spanish name."

"But 'Isabella' isn't on your birth certificate, is it?" Cathy asked.

"No, it's just plain 'Izzy'."

"I quite like the name. I think I'll call you 'Isabella' from now on."

"In that case, I'll call you 'Catherine'," she said laughing.

"I can't wait to tell George! I was just telling him where we've been today."

"Wait! You haven't heard the strangest bit yet: Henry George Derwin - married to Catherine."

"Yes?" Cathy said.

"What is your George's middle name?"

"Henry…" Cathy replied, as the penny dropped.

"Yes! Is that not the weirdest thing? What are the chances of that happening? And you are moving into your (I don't know how many greats it would be) grandparents' place, five hundred years later. Spooky!"

"So my ancestor was hanged?" Cathy asked.

"I wouldn't worry about history repeating itself. They don't hang them anymore," Izzy said, laughing.

"I'll see you tomorrow, then. Bye Izzy," she said, cheerfully.

"I take it that was Izzy?" George asked.

"Yes, you know what she's like, being meticulous about detail and always taking notes at night school? Well, you wait till you hear this! I am a *direct descendant* of *Henry Derwin*, who was *hanged*."

"Oh yes, you said he lived at the cottage."

Cathy related the rest of the conversation to George, expecting him to be as excited as she was.

"That sounds like Izzy for you, making something out of nothing," George replied, drily.

"Well, I thought it was all highly significant!" Cathy said, disappointed at his reaction.

"Yes, dear, if you say so."

"You never take things seriously, George."

"Talking of serious things, I've got the conference starting tomorrow. I won't be back for a few days; are you going to be alright?"

"Of course, I will! I'm pregnant, not an invalid!"

"You look as though you've had a bad day, darling," George said as he looked at Cathy, who was collapsed in a heap on the sofa.

"You can say that again!" Cathy replied, tiredly.

"You look as though you've had a bad day, darling."

"Oh, that is all I need! Some of your schoolboy humour to make me feel better. For goodness sake, grow up, George!"

Taken aback by the disdain in Cathy's voice, George became concerned. This was so unlike her. But then, he reflected, she was probably tired and her hormones might be affecting her, if what he'd heard about pregnant women was true. "Sorry, dear. Now I really am worried that you're overdoing things. You must take more care of yourself! Why don't you stay at home tomorrow and put your feet up. I could even take a day off and spoil you."

"Thanks, George, but I really need to be at the cottage. Things won't sort themselves out."

"What are you talking about?"

"I've been having problems with the tradesmen."

"What do you mean, 'problems'?" he asked, concerned.

"The plasterer was only upstairs for an hour before he came down looking pale. He said he couldn't work there and when I asked him why, he shook his head. Then I asked if it was the money and he said, "Lady, you couldn't pay me enough to work here!" and just left.

Then the electrician didn't turn up the next morning. I phoned to see where he was and all he said was that he couldn't work in such a place. Before I had a chance to ask what he meant, he hung up!

Still, I'm pleased to say the thatcher's finished, and I've managed to get another plasterer and electrician. The plumbing's all done and so is the plastering. I never did find out what was wrong with the first lot.

It's just the electrician to get done now. I told him where I wanted all the lights and wall sockets yesterday and he knows where to get hold of me if there's a problem."

"So, I take it all's okay now?"

"Well, I hope so. Apparently the electrician had been having trouble with the nursery room. The lights kept flashing on and off all day. He said he couldn't figure it out, as the next day it was fine. Still, he assures me the wiring is safe in the room."

"I suppose you're itching to make a start on the place, with Izzy?"

"Do you know, I really am! I think the electrician will be finished tomorrow and we can get on with it. Now, how was your conference?"

"All ready, Izzy? I brought some lunch for us and some milk to make coffee."

As they pulled up outside Izzy remarked, "Wow! doesn't the new thatch make it look different?"

"Now all the plastering's been done, it looks different inside as well," Cathy said, opening the front door.

"That new cooking range looks the part!" remarked Izzy. "Are we making a start in here first?"

"No, I thought the attic rooms. What do you think?"

"I suppose it's as good a place as any. Start at the top and work down? Yes?"

"Come on then, let's go up," Cathy replied, leading the way.

Arriving in the furthest room, Izzy asked, "What do you want done to the ceiling beams - painted or scrubbed down?"

"Scrubbed! I want to bring this place back to it's original condition, or as near as possible," Cathy replied. "I can imagine lots of children sleeping up here, can't you, Izzy?"

"It must have been draughty and cold for them. But then I suppose they were used to it, not knowing any different," Izzy replied. "Cathy, I wonder when these little windows were added."

I'm not sure, but they're definitely not original. They wouldn't have had windows in the attic. Probably last century, but I haven't a clue why, as nobody has lived up here for *years*."

"Maybe the old lady had them done to make the place look nice from the outside, and now the thatch has been done, it sure does that, Cathy."

"Look at the character of this beam, with all its split grain and knots. I so love the way they fixed these beams to one another with dowels," Cathy said.

131

As she started to scrub around one of the large wooden dowels, she noticed that it was protruding more than the others and was loose. "I have a loose dowel over here, Izzy. I'd better try to bang it back in."

"Here, give it a tap with the hammer," Izzy said, passing one to her.

"It keeps bouncing out. There must be something stopping it," Cathy said, frowning. She gripped the stub of dowel with her fingers and pulled it out. Peering into the hole, she said, "I think there's something squashed in there. Pass me that long, thin screwdriver, Izzy."

Izzy watched Cathy pull out a small package tied with twine. "What is it, Cathy?"

Cathy climbed down from the stepladder and took it under the light. She gently pulled one end of the twine, and unfolded the scrap of rag. "It's a little beaded band," she said.

"There's something embroidered on the rag, Cathy."

*To my best friend, Catherine,
lest we forget each other.
May our friendship go on forever.
Isabella.'*

"It must have been there for hundreds of years. It's obvious that it was hidden, but I wonder why," Cathy said.

"We'll never know, Cathy, but isn't it strange that Isabella and Catherine were best friends like us. What will you do with it?"

"It's so beautiful; I think I'm going to put it on display in a little glass box. It'll add to the charm and make a great talking point when we have visitors."

"Good day, dear?" George asked, as he sat down to wait for supper.

"An exciting day! The cottage has given up one of its secrets. I found a little friendship bracelet hidden in a beam and there was a message with it," she said, showing him.

"Knowing you, you're probably going to keep it somewhere?"

"Of course!"

"So how far did you get today?" he asked.

"Well, we've finished one of the attic rooms and made a start on the other. Hopefully, it'll be finished by tomorrow night and then we'll tackle the nursery. Who knows what we might find hidden!"

"You say that as if you're expecting to find something."

"Funny you should say that, George. I can't explain it, but there's something about the place; it's as if I was meant to be there. Even Izzy, the first time she set foot in there, had a feeling that she'd been there before, and now I'm feeling it too."

"Well, you know my views on subjects like that. I honestly think that it's your love for period places that's taken over the two of you. Still, if you're enjoying yourself, that's all that matters," George replied.

"Thank you, dear," Cathy said, rolling her eyes.

The phone rang, and they both looked at each other, waiting to see who was going to get up and answer it.

"It's bound to be for you; Izzy probably," George said, nudging her to get up. Cathy picked up the phone, thinking he was likely to be right.

"Mrs Dawson? Father Michael here. We met at the church the other day."

"Of course, Father, how can I help you?"

"I do apologise, but the estate agent (rather reluctantly) gave me your number. Actually, I wondered if you would mind asking your friend, Izzy, if she'd drop by the church when she's out this way. There's something I'd like to show her – I believe it'll be of interest."

Cathy stood there looking at the handset not believing that she didn't get a chance to pry any more information out of him before he'd hung up.

"Who was that then? George asked, "I know it wasn't Izzy by the length of the call."

"No, it was the priest we visited, with a message for Izzy. I can't wait to tell her tomorrow."

"Why wait till tomorrow? You know you're itching to tell her. Anyway, there's a programme I want to watch; it's about to start," he said reaching for the remote.

Cathy immediately dialled Izzy and told her about the call.

"It sounds intriguing!"

"What about if you drive tomorrow and drop me off at the cottage, then you can go on to meet him?"

"If you're sure you'll be alright on your own. I must confess I can't wait to find out what he wants to show me."

"Of course I will; I shouldn't think you'll be that long. I'll only be stripping wallpaper in the nursery. I'll see you in the morning, usual time. Don't forget, Izzy, *you're* picking *me* up."

"As they pulled up outside the cottage, Izzy said, "I should think I'll be about an hour. Are you sure now that you're going to be okay on your own?"

"Yes, now stop talking and go!" Cathy replied.

"No climbing step ladders!" Izzy called through window as she drove off.

Izzy went round to the rear of the church and knocked on the door, but there didn't seem to be anyone in. Just as she was about to walk away the door opened.

"Sorry about that, I was on the phone. How can I help you?"

"I'm Izzy. My friend, Cathy Dawson, said that you wanted to see me, Father."

"Ah! Yes, thank you for coming. I thought I'd better not wait until you happened to call again. After you left last time, I came across another ancient book. It contained the personal writings of a 'Father Joel' who was the priest here in 1513. Look, I think it would be easier to show you, rather than try to tell you."

She followed him into the vestry where he took both books out of the chest. He turned to the page in Father Joel's book that he wanted to show her.

"Start reading from here. Are you okay with old English writing?" he asked her.

"Oh yes! We came across it during a course that Cathy and I went on," she replied.

"Okay, if you read from here, 13th February, to there," he said pointing. "See if you notice anything unusual."

Having read the entries, Izzy looked up and said, "All the dates start with the number thirteen?"

"Yes! But it was the entry of the 13th of April, when an exorcism was performed at the cottage, that I am concerned about."

Puzzled, Izzy asked, "Why would that make you concerned? Surely, once an exorcism is performed, it gets rid of anything that was supposedly evil?"

"Yes, normally it does but, reading on, he says on the 13th May: *'A heavy burden lies within my soul that the evil spirit in the room is not at rest. But, by the grace of God, the door to the room has been boarded up, which is now the only containment of the evil spirit that lies within. God*

135

help anyone living in such a place if the boarding were to be removed, for who could stand such evil that would be unleashed?"

"Yes, I read that. So, are you saying there's still an evil spirit in the place?" she asked, alarmed.

"I'm not sure, but there seem to have been a lot of deaths there. Did you notice the entry for the 12th April?"

"Yes, Tobias Spry and his curse?" she said with a chuckle.

"You should take this seriously. A curse spoken out in those days was powerful. Because people believed in them, as they do today in some countries, they were effective."

"So who was Tobias Spry then?" Izzy asked.

"He must have been someone who was known to be involved in the occult. You see his words were probably unquestioned and feared by most people."

"But why would he have placed a curse? You would have thought he wanted to be left alone to get on with his dark practices," Izzy reasoned.

"You obviously missed that line. Father Joel mentioned why Tobias Spry spoke it out. If what he says is true, then the curse was directed at Daniel Derwin and all his descendants. As far as we know, no one has died in all those centuries since Father Joel wrote this, but I've begun to have suspicions about Mrs Myrtle's death."

"Oh, yes, wasn't that the old lady who last lived there?"

"It was, and, having read up on these things, it was most probably a hex."

"A hex?"

"Yes, apparently a hex is a powerful negative thought expressed with a strong emotional outburst. It's thought by some that the more energy used in the ritual of hexing, the more effective the hex will be upon the recipient. It is said that when the subconscious mind is convinced that something will happen, the fear and negative emotions make any curse or hex work.

I think Tobias Spry's life must have been threatened by Daniel Derwin, or something like that. The mystery is though, what connection Tobias Spry had with the cottage. The records show he didn't live there, nor indeed did he live anywhere in the parish. I tried to find more information from Father Joel's book but there were no more entries concerning the cottage. The church records show that Father Joel died in 1553," Father Michael said.

"Didn't it say that Henry Derwin lived in the cottage? Maybe he was Daniel Derwin's son?"

"If he was, it might explain why he died, and two of his children, so close to each other. Disconcertingly, according to Father Joel, the curse is still active," he replied.

"Well, we know that his wife and remaining children had to leave because it was a tied cottage, but do you think the curse followed them?" Izzy asked.

"Hard to say, but it did say he cursed Derwin and his descendants. We'll never know what happened to them," he said, shaking his head.

"Are you sure there aren't any more references to the cottage throughout the centuries?" she asked.

"As far as I can see, nothing untoward, but, as I said the other day, record-keeping was somewhat hit and miss back then. All that's entered here concerns Miriam Myrtle - when she moved into the cottage and then again when she died."

"Oh, what dates are they?" Izzy asked.

"It says that she and her husband moved into the cottage in 1913…."

"There's that *thirteen* again," Izzy interrupted.

"But he died not long after, lost in action during the war. She's lived there ever since, well, until about five years ago, when she died."

"Yes, I remember - you found her at the bottom of the stairs. Didn't you say that she told you about voices upstairs?"

"Yes, she did, but at the time I just thought it was her old age."

"Father Michael, what was the date she died?"

There was silence as he looked at the entry date. "The 13th March!"

"So, somewhere in the cottage there's a door that's been boarded up? I was just going to say: maybe that's why there weren't any more reports of deaths, but if the old lady's death on the 13th isn't a coincidence, then the boarding isn't making any difference."

"It sounds that way. Have you seen boarding in any of the rooms or felt anything strange - like an uneasiness?" he asked.

"We've only just started on the place; I haven't noticed any boarding and, no, I've not really sensed anything wrong there," she replied.

"You say 'not really'; it sounds as if you're not sure?" he probed.

"It's probably nothing, but when Cathy was showing me around, the minute I walked into one of the bedrooms I felt an overwhelming sense of sadness in there, but not fear. Funnily enough, I did discuss it with Cathy - saying that it might be that I was picking up on past events that had gone on in that room."

"Tell me, Izzy, was the room in the right hand side of the cottage?"

"You know, Father Michael, it was! That would have been the Derwin's cottage, as it was then, wouldn't it?"

"Yes," he said, deep in thought, "It would have been."

138

"I can't help wondering why the old lady died there. Was it just due to natural causes or was it linked with the supposed curse or something? After all, her name wasn't 'Derwin' so I don't see how the curse could have affected her," Izzy reasoned.

"Well, if it wasn't a natural death, I think the only explanation is that somewhere behind the wall boarding (if it still exists) is the source of the evil that affects anyone living there. But the curse is something different; it is on the *name*: Derwin. There would be no escape from it," he replied.

"Father Michael, do you remember Cathy saying that her family name was Derwin? Well I traced her family history back and it appears that she is a direct descendant of Henry Derwin. If his father was Daniel, then Cathy would be cursed. I wish she was here, hearing all this. She's alone in that place and, if all we've spoken about is true, anything could happen to her."

"You should get back as quickly as you can! I was going to say that I would like to see the room some time, but because of what you told me and today's date, I feel that I should come with you now," he said urgently.

"What is the date?" she asked.

"Today is the 13th and it's not just any 13th; it's *Friday* the 13th. If anything happens, it seems from past history that it happens on the 13th."

"I don't agree with superstition, Father Michael, but I must admit there does seem to be something strange about the number 13 and the cottage," she replied.

"Nor do I, but you must understand the place was built in a time when it *was* what they believed in. The whole cottage has been soaked with superstition and, even though centuries have come and gone, it could be that which is keeping the evil alive in the cottage today. Do you believe in prayer, Izzy?"

139

"Yes, I do, but I'm not sure about Cathy. We've both recently started going to church – but not a Catholic one (sorry, Father!)."

"Then pray, Izzy. Pray for your friend - that she will have God's protection over her and that it's not too late."

"Yes, of course. I must ring her to tell her to get out of the place. Oh no, it's gone to voice mail!"

She left a desperate message: "Cathy, if you get this message, get out of the house! Get out!"

17

Cathy was making steady progress stripping wallpaper and had only the wall near the chimneybreast to do. Having run out of water, she went to the bathroom down the hall to fill the bucket and, while in there, she heard voices. Thinking it was Izzy, and that she'd brought someone with her, she called out, "Izzy, did you think of getting milk?" But there was no answer. Assuming Izzy hadn't heard, she made her way back with the water. As she stepped into the room, the words: "Izzy, did you get . . .", were stopped short, as there was no one in the room.

Puzzled, she shrugged her shoulders and set about sponging the wallpaper, then let it soak for a while, as she pondered on the voices. Did she imagine them? The first strip came off easily, revealing a section of old pine boards. Her eyes were drawn to many scriptures written in ink over the boards. As the windows were small and didn't let in much light, she turned on the electric light, to see more clearly what she had uncovered. Encouraged by the find, she removed the rest of the paper from the boards, which were also covered in scripture. Some of them where written in italic lettering, telling her that they were probably centuries old, and the others were in more modern writing. She noticed that they were all scriptures of protection from evil. She started to read them out loud, and, as she did so, the lights started to flash on and off. She paused for a moment, looking up at the lights, but remembering the electrician's assurance that it was safe, she continued.

'I pray not that thou shouldest take them out of the world, but that thou shouldest keep them from evil.' John 17:15

But the Lord is faithful, who shall establish you, and keep you from evil.
2 Thessalonians 3:3

'We know that whosoever is born of God sinneth not; but he that is begotten of God keepeth himself, and that the wicked one toucheth him not.' 1 John 5:18

'Yea, though I walk through the valley of the shadow of death, I will fear no evil: for thou art with me; thy rod and thy staff they comfort me.' Psalm 23:4

Because thou hast made the Lord, which is my refuge, even the most high, thy habitation; there shall no evil befall thee, neither shall any plague come nigh thy dwelling, for he shall give his angels charge over thee, to keep thee in all thy ways.'
Psalms 91:9 :11

Cathy's phone made a beep, causing her to stop reading. She could see she had a voice mail from Izzy but all she could hear was the word 'get', and the rest was distorted by static. She walked around the house, trying to get a clearer signal, but because that didn't help, she decided to go out the back of the house.

Izzy's car came to a screeching halt on the gravel drive, followed by Father Michael in his car. Not even closing the car door, Izzy ran into the house and up the stairs, calling, "Cathy, Cathy!" Father Michael followed close behind, panting. Izzy ran into the room where she knew Cathy would be, but was alarmed to find she wasn't there. Her eyes went to the boards and the scriptures.

"Is this the room?" Father Michael asked.

"Yes!" she said as she rushed out, leaving him there. She ran down the hallway, checking the other room and frantically calling out. She stopped at the base of the attic stairs and shouted, "Are you up there, Cathy?" There was an ominous silence.

Then a thought came to her. *Maybe she got the message and did get out of the house.* As she didn't see her when she arrived, she assumed she was somewhere out the back. She looked out of the window and, to her relief, there was Cathy walking around with the phone to her ear!

Opening the window, she called out, "Cathy, stay there – I'm coming down!" She sped down the stairs and rushed outside. "Are you all right? I was worried about you!"

Of course I am. I couldn't hear your message because of this awful static. I'm sure there's something wrong with the signal in the house."

"So you haven't heard my message then?" Izzy asked.

"No, that's what I'm saying. Why? Was it important?"

"Thank God, you're out here!" she said, hugging her.

"What's going on?" asked Cathy, puzzled.

"I'm just pleased to see you," said Izzy, instantly deciding not to alarm her.

"You wait till I show you what I found upstairs!" Cathy said, taking Izzy's hand and leading her towards the house. "I thought you came back earlier. I could have sworn I heard someone talking, but I must have imagined it."

Izzy, thinking about the old lady who heard voices upstairs, quickly changed the subject. She said, "I brought Father Michael back with me; he's upstairs."

"Oh, did you?" Cathy said. "Let's go back in – I'm sure he'll be interested in what I've found too."

Father Michael stood facing the wall, reading the scriptures. Suddenly the room was filled with violent banging, followed by what sounded like a desperate scream from behind the wooden boarding. He stepped back in shock, feeling as though he was about to have a heart attack. In disbelief he could see the boarding starting to bow outwards towards him and then back, prising the nails from the boards.

"Holy Mother of God!" he cried out as he turned and ran for the door, but it slammed shut before he could reach it.

As he tried to turn the doorknob, to his horror, he found it wouldn't turn. With both hands, he tried with all his might, but something stronger held it from turning. Then suddenly the banging and screaming stopped. He slowly turned round to see smoke coming from beneath the boarding. It was rapidly filling the room and starting to make him choke. Panic-stricken, he tried to get out, banging on the door and desperately hoping Izzy would hear his cries. The acrid smoke quickly filled his lungs and he slithered to the floor as he gasped for breath.

144

"So, where is he?" Cathy asked, as they made their way up the stairs.

"I left him in here," Izzy said as they stood outside the nursery. "Father Michael, can we come in?" she called.

But there was no answer. Izzy turned the doorknob but found that the door only opened a little way as there was something stopping it from opening.

"There's something blocking the door, Cathy. Can you push with me?"

As they both heaved, it began to move just enough for Izzy to put her head round the door to see what the obstruction was.

"Father Michael!" she cried out. "Push, Cathy. It's Father Michael - he's collapsed behind the door!"

The door slowly eased open, wide enough for them to squeeze through.

"Is he okay?" Cathy asked.

Izzy crouched down, feeling for a pulse. "No, Cathy he's not. I think he's dead."

"Dead! How?" Cathy said in disbelief.

"I don't know. He was all right when I left him here. It's only been a matter of minutes!" Izzy replied, just as shocked as Cathy.

"Maybe he's had a heart attack; he looks awfully white," Cathy said. "I'll stay here with him, Izzy, and you go outside and ring the police."

"No! I'm not leaving you here on your own; we'll go together," Izzy replied.

"Don't be silly! I'm all right. I don't mind being alone with a dead body – don't forget I used to work in a hospice at one time. The dead can't hurt you," Cathy replied.

Izzy knew she couldn't take any chances, after what had just happened to Father Michael. "Even so, you're coming with me. It'll make me feel better."

"Okay, but I feel we should come back up here to be with him. It's the least we can do for him until the police get here."

As they came back into the room, Cathy said, "Izzy, is it my imagination or is there a faint smell of smoke in here – as though a bonfire's been burning?"

Izzy sniffed the air as she walked around the room. "I was thinking that, when I came into the room. She followed the smell, sniffing as she went. "It's stronger here by the door." Bending down she smelt Father Michael's clothes. "His clothes reek of smoke, Cathy!"

"Maybe he's been burning stuff at the churchyard," Cathy said.

"No, I would have smelt it earlier when I was with him, and I didn't see any bonfires there. I just don't know, Cathy," Izzy replied, perplexed.

"You never did tell me what he wanted to see you about," Cathy said.

"Can I tell you later? I don't think this is the right time or place. What was it you found that you were going to show me?" Izzy said, hoping Cathy would drop the subject as she didn't want to say anything until she'd figured out how to go about it.

"Oh, yes - over here! There are lots of old scriptures all over the boarding," she said as she crossed the room to show Izzy.

"Yes, I saw them when I was looking for you, but I haven't had a chance to read them."

"Do you think that's what Father Michael was doing in the room before he died?"

"He might have done, Cathy. After all, it would be nice to think that was the last thing he did."

"Did you notice what all the scriptures have in common, Izzy?"

146

Izzy studied them. "Protection," she said.

"Yes, that's what I thought, protection from evil. But why would whoever wrote them need protection from evil?" Cathy replied.

"It's what they were taught. Remember, it was a time when people were steeped in religion," Izzy replied.

"Yes, I understand all that but, if you look, you can tell some of the scriptures are more recent by the writing."

"Maybe the old lady who lived here was religious," Izzy said.

They were both relieved to hear the sound of car tyres stopping on the gravel outside. Looking out of the window, Izzy said, "That was quick! It's the police – we'd better go down and let them in."

"Mrs Dawson, you reported a death?"

Cathy led the officer and his colleague upstairs, with Izzy following behind.

She showed them into the room where Father Michael lay on the floor.

The officer bent down to check his pulse, then standing up he said, "Can you tell me what happened, and the relationship between you and him?"

"His name is Father Michael; he came here a short while ago with my friend, Izzy, but I've only met him once before."

Izzy filled them in with more detail. "Was it his heart?" she added.

"I can't say; that's a job for the medics, who should be here soon. If you two could go back downstairs with my colleague, I'll be down in a minute."

The officer soon came down into the room where Cathy and Izzy were sitting.

147

"There's an awful lot of static here, stopping me phoning to see were the medics are. I'll go out to the car radio to make the call," the office said to his colleague.

"Fine, I'll take some notes here," he replied. "Can we go over how you know the deceased again and what he was doing here, while we wait for the paramedics," the officer said, taking his note pad out.

"How long before you remove him, once they get here?" Izzy asked.

"Couldn't say. It all depends on whether they come across anything out of the ordinary, in which case they'll send for the coroner, and that may take some time," the officer replied.

"Out of the ordinary – like what?" Izzy asked.

"They will be checking to see if he could have been resuscitated or not. Did you try to resuscitate him?"

"Well no. I checked his pulse and could see he was already dead. It wouldn't have been any use," Cathy said.

"It will probably be straight forward and the medics will remove him, but we will have to wait and see if they're satisfied that no foul play was involved."

"Is it okay if we phone our husbands in case there is a delay? They'll be expecting us home soon," Izzy asked.

While they were outside on their phones, they saw the medics arrive, and then taken into the house by the officer.

"This is awful, Izzy! Do you think he has a wife, or family?" Cathy said as they went back into the house.

"I know; you just don't expect things like this to happen. I'm not sure if they are allowed to marry, but he might have family somewhere. I'm sure the police will find out. He seemed such a nice man. Did you manage to speak to George?" Izzy asked.

"No; as usual, he's in a meeting. I left a message for him to ring me. What about you?"

"Voice mail; I left a message saying I'll be home late."

"Looks as if they're all upstairs," she said, referring to the officers and medics. "I hope they don't find any problems with his death, Izzy."

Izzy was hoping the same, but deep down she had a nagging feeling that he died the same way as all the others in the past - by something evil in the room. "Let's hope so Cathy," she replied.

As they entered the room, the officer asked: "Mrs Dawson, how long before you phoned us, after you found him dead?"

"As soon as we found him, plus the time it took us to go back outside to get a signal - say five minutes."

"So how long from when you left him in the room, would you say, to when you found him?" he asked. Cathy looked at Izzy to answer.

"Ten to fifteen minutes at the most. Why? Is there a problem?" Izzy asked him.

One of the paramedics spoke quietly into the officer's ear, which irritated Izzy, who was anxious to know what he was saying.

"Mrs Dawson, we seem to have a problem here. You stated, or your friend here," looking at the note book, he said, "Mrs Earnshaw, stated that it was ten to fifteen minutes at the most from when you saw him alive to when you found him dead?"

"That's right," Izzy said.

"Well the paramedics here say that's impossible, as full rigor mortis has set in, and that starts three hours after death, with complete stiffness in twelve hours. So, you see, there is a discrepancy with what you've told us. Can you explain it?"

"I'm not qualified on the subject of rigor mortis, or how that can be, but all I know is what we have told you is the truth. One minute he was alive and then he was dead," Izzy said emphatically.

"Mrs Dawson, I'm afraid this might take some time." With that the officer made his way outside followed by the paramedics, leaving the other officer with them.

"What's going to happen now?" Izzy asked.

"We will have to wait while my colleague requests the coroner to attend."

Getting up from the chair, Izzy said, "Look! We've done nothing wrong here!"

"Then you have nothing to worry about, Mrs Earnshaw. Please sit down."

"I've just realised, Izzy; I left a message for George to ring me back, but as there's no signal in here, he won't be able to, and I didn't say anything about what's happened."

"I would try again later, Cathy; anyway I'm sure we'll be home soon."

"The coroner will be about an hour," the officer said to his colleague as he came in.

After a few minutes, Izzy broke the silence: "Would you two like a cup of tea or coffee?"

"Thank you, that's good of you, I'll have tea if that's alright."

"Yes tea's fine for me too," the other officer replied.

"Looks as if you're going to have a nice place here when it's finished. How old is it?"

"Thank you, it's about sixteenth century. There's still lots to do, but I didn't reckon on something like this happening," Cathy replied.

"I'm sure it will all be sorted out when the coroner gets here, Mrs Dawson; then you can get back to your renovating," the officer said, trying to reassure her.

As Izzy passed them tea, there was a sound like muffled voices upstairs, causing them all to look at each other, puzzled.

"Is there anyone else here with the two of you?" one of the policemen asked.

"No, just us," Izzy said, sounding alarmed.

The officers put their cups down and made their way up the stairs, followed by Izzy and Cathy. They could hear the muffled voices coming from behind the door of the room where Father Michael lay dead. The leading officer turned the doorknob and started to open it, but as they stepped into the room the voices stopped abruptly. They could only look at one another in bewilderment, as did Cathy and Izzy, looking from the doorway.

"Hello!" a voice called up the stairs, "It's the coroner."

"Up here!" called out one of the men.

"What have we here?" the coroner asked, turning on the light.

"A 'Father Michael'. It appears that he was left alone in the room until Mrs Dawson and Mrs Earnshaw found him dead; they say some fifteen minutes later.

"Can we clear the room, officer? I need to examine him."

One of the officers led Cathy and Izzy downstairs, while the coroner set to work.

"You say he was found some fifteen minutes after they last saw him alive?"

"That's the statement they made; the paramedics suspected something wrong with the timing as full rigor mortis had set in," answered the officer.

"Yes, indeed; it appears so. Can you give me a hand to turn him on his back?"

As they turned him over, they saw on his chest a bloodstained handprint. The light began to flicker on and off violently, causing them both to look up.

"Dodgy wiring in these old places," the officer said.

"This looks interesting," the coroner said as he peered over the glasses on the end of his nose. "I need to get him back to the morgue; can you ask the paramedics to come up?"

Cathy and Izzy sat at the table as they watched the body of Father Michael taken out of the house.

"Can we go home now?" Izzy asked the officers.

"Yes, but we will need to speak to you both soon," said the officer.

"Sure, no problem," replied Izzy.

"What do we do with Father Michael's car outside?" Cathy asked.

"We will arrange for it to be taken away," the officer replied. "Oh, by the way, you've got some dodgy wiring in that room; I'd get it fixed if I was you. We wouldn't want anymore deaths," the officer said, going out of the door.

"Dodgy wiring? I thought you'd just had it all rewired?" Izzy said, frowning.

"Yes. I had a problem as well with the lights flashing on and off earlier. I'll get the electrician back to sort it out." Closing the cottage door, Cathy said, "What a day that was! I'm glad it's over; let's go home."

"And they say the 13th isn't unlucky!" Izzy said.

"I didn't realise it was the 13th today, but what are you doing, believing that thirteen is unlucky? I thought you weren't superstitious!"

"I'm not, it's just that ...."

"Just what, Izzy?"

"Nothing. You're not working tomorrow are you?" she said, quickly changing the subject.

"No, weekend off. George is taking me away; he likes to spoil me," Cathy replied.

"What - you're missing church on Sunday?"

"It's not my fault, it's George's."

"Yes, sure."

Cathy gave a smug little smile. "Say 'hello' to Pastor Peter for me."

"Yes, okay. Well, here we are," Izzy said, pulling up outside Cathy's home. "Have a good time with George, I'll ring you Monday."

George had already poured himself a glass of wine by the time Cathy arrived home.

"Sorry I'm late, darling. You won't believe what happened today!" she announced.

"Don't tell me! You and Izzy found bats or something in the cottage."

"Oh, George, this is serious! The priest visited us today and we found him *dead* in one of the rooms! We think he must have had a heart attack or something."

"Oh, my goodness! Sit down, dear. You've had a nasty shock. Why on earth was he visiting?"

"Well, I suppose we're going to be in his parish – or were. I think he was interested in the history of the place too. Anyway, we had to call the police and everything."

"It's a good job we're going away for the weekend, then. It'll be good for you to relax and take your mind of it all."

18

"Good morning Izzy, no husband or Cathy with you?" Pastor Peter asked her.

"No, he's at home. Although he doesn't mind me coming, he says it's not for him. And Cathy's being spoilt by her husband. He's taken her away for the weekend. She asked me to say 'hi' to you."

"Well, I hope she has a nice time," he replied, smiling.

"Knowing Cathy, she'll make sure she does! Pastor Peter, I need to have a chat with you; is it possible to speak to you after the service?" Izzy asked.

"Of course, you know I'm always here for you and it will be good to get to know you a bit better."

After the service, Izzy sat at a table drinking coffee while waiting for Pastor Peter to say his farewells to the people. This was an ideal opportunity to speak to the pastor about the cottage now Cathy was away.

"Thanks for being patient, Izzy; now about that chat," Pastor Peter said, sitting down next to her. "How are you finding it here, now you've been coming for a few weeks?"

"I love it! Everyone is so friendly and welcoming. I must admit I thought churches were cold, depressing places where only a few elderly folk attended, but this church is so lively and packed with people of all ages."

"So what made you come in the first place?"

"Well, both Cathy and I felt there must be more to life. We both had wonderful lives with adoring husbands and lovely homes, yet there was something missing that neither of us could explain – a kind of emptiness. Then a leaflet about the church meetings came through my letterbox and we felt we should give it a try."

"I'm glad you did. A lot of people look to fill that emptiness with things that seem appealing, but that only bring them harm."

"What do you mean?"

"Drugs, alcohol, gambling, to name a few. Take me for instance – I was once a hopeless addict, living on the streets and stealing to feed my habit. It was only when I reached rock bottom that I would admit I needed help. And when I did call out to God, he transformed my life. I couldn't be happier now."

"*Wow!* I would never have believed that if you hadn't told me yourself."

"Believe it. I was the worst of the worst; you couldn't get any lower. I was in prison more than once. Anyway, enough about me - what did you want to chat about?"

"Well, you've heard that Cathy has bought an old cottage?"

"Yes, she was telling me about it last Sunday. She sounded quite excited about it, and, I must say, it sounds very nice."

"I'm not sure where to start. I've found out something about the history of the cottage that's quite worrying; and I don't know how to tell her without destroying her dream of living there. I was hoping, Pastor, that you could give me some advice."

"It sounds mysterious! Why don't you start from the beginning, Izzy? It's usually a good place to start."

Izzy told him all that she had found out and what had happened to the priest.

"Well, I must confess it does sound a little far fetched, but there do seem to be a lot of coincidences with this number 13. I know that superstition can create fear and maybe that's part of the problem."

"Yes, Father Michael said something like that," Izzy replied. "But do you believe such a thing as a *curse* is real?"

"Absolutely. The Bible says a lot about curses."

"Really?" said Izzy, shocked. "Where?"

"You don't have to look far. The first time a curse is mentioned is right at the beginning – in Genesis 3. God created a world that was perfect and beautiful. The first people, Adam and Eve lacked nothing and could have experienced Heaven on Earth if they hadn't disobeyed God."

"Yes, Pastor, but I've always found it quite hard to understand. It seems a bit harsh to throw them out of the Garden because they disobeyed over *one thing*."

"Well, he only asked them to obey him over *one thing*."

"But was that really so bad? I mean, it was only eating fruit wasn't it?"

"It was a lot more than that, Izzy. By obeying Satan and ignoring what God said, they were handing their authority over the earth to Satan, which meant the earth became cursed. That's the reason we have sickness and disease, crime, wars, hatred, cruelty, oppression, the list goes on."

"So, a curse is when Satan has authority over someone?"

"He has authority over *everyone* (until they choose otherwise). Everyone is destined for Hell when they die. It's the most terrible place and there's no going back. But, thank God, we can escape it."

"Yes – if you're a good person and if you go to church?"

"No! Izzy, I've preached over and over again about this, but I know you're quite new to the church. *No one* is good enough and there's nothing anyone can do to make themselves good by God's standards."

"So *how* do we escape Hell? I thought I was doing okay."

"Jesus paid the price that we can't pay. He suffered terrible agony on the cross and rose from he dead so that we all could live for eternity with him in Heaven, instead of spending eternity in Hell."

"So, you're now saying we'll *all* go to Heaven because of Jesus."

"No, it's not automatic. It is a gift, but we have to actually *receive* it. Most people ignore the offer, even though it's free."

"How do you mean 'receive' it? I don't get it?'

"You tell him that you want to. The Bible says: *'If you confess with your mouth, "Jesus is Lord", and believe in your heart that God raised him from the dead, you will be saved."*

"So why doesn't everyone do that?" Or why doesn't God make them?"

"Satan has blinded most people to the truth – he's even convinced most of them that he doesn't even exist. And God would never force himself on anyone. He wants them to be free to *choose* him, just as you wouldn't want anyone to be forced to marry you."

"In a way it sounds too good to be true – accepting a free gift. It's something I need to think about. It's a bit scary, making that decision."

"It's a lot more scary *not* making it!"

"Because of not going to Heaven?"

"Yes, partly, but once you've made that commitment you can have a wonderful life on earth – filled with joy, peace and even excitement."

"Going back to the 'curse': if we're all cursed already, how can a person be 'under a curse' or a place be cursed?"

"Well, apart from the original curse I was talking about, people can open themselves to curses in their lives (or put curses on others) by involvement in occult practices for instance. Some, although not all, are unaware of the evil they are dealing with."

"Do you believe in exorcism, Pastor Peter?"

"Well yes, but I have only experienced it concerning people, not properties. Even though, from what you've told me about Cathy's cottage, I'm not sure the place will need anything like that."

"I don't know; I'm so concerned for Cathy living there. Would you come and visit the place, and maybe you can see if you sense anything there," Izzy said.

"Let me know when, Izzy, and I'll see if I can arrange it. I must confess I wouldn't mind seeing the place, especially the old scriptures" he replied.

"So, do you think I should tell Cathy?"

"Well, that's really up to you; I can't say, but I will visit the place, and we'll go from there."

"Thank you Pastor Peter, I'll arrange it with Cathy and ring you."

"I'll look forward to hearing from you."

Cathy pulled up outside Izzy's place and sounded the horn. Izzy soon came running out to the car and, before she even had her seat belt on, said: "Come on then, tell me what did you get up to?"

"Five star hotel with health centre, gorgeous food and expensive wine," Cathy replied.

"Horrible time then?" Izzy said, smiling.

"What did you get up to?"

"Shopping therapy - Saturday, church - Sunday. Pastor Peter says he hoped you would have a nice time. By the way, you won't believe this! He used to be a drug addict and he's been in prison!" said Izzy.

"You're kidding! I thought people like that grew up as goody-goodies. How do you know that?"

"He told me. We got talking after church about your place and the scriptures you uncovered. He says he would like to come and see them, so I said I'd speak to you about it and let him know when he could."

"You know what happened the last time you brought someone from the church to see the place!" Cathy said.

"Because Father Michael died from a heat attack, doesn't mean that something's going to happen to Pastor Peter," Izzy replied.

"We don't know yet if it was his heart, do we?"

Cathy's statement, made Izzy think about what she knew. By inviting Pastor Peter to the house, would she be putting him in danger? Her mind went back to the church visit with Father Michael. She could hear his words: *"There seems to be a great significance with the number 13 - that if anything is going to happen it seems from past history that it happens on the 13th."* Based on that, he would be safe to visit on any other day.

"*Do* we Izzy?"

"Sorry Cathy, I was miles away then. Er... no."

"You're doing a lot of that lately. Of course it would be nice for him to visit; I'd love to show him round. You say he wants to see the scriptures?" Cathy asked.

"Yes," that bit was true, but she still couldn't bring herself to tell her the real reason she wanted him there. Deep down it was upsetting her, keeping things from her best friend.

"What about a month's time, that'll give us time to finish the upstairs, then we'll have something to show him?" Cathy said.

Izzy reckoned quickly - a month would take it too near the 13th so, to play safe, she said, "I think he wanted it sooner than later, being busy with the church. I know you would like it all to be finished, Cathy, but I'm sure he would like to see it as it is, and anyway, you might have decided to cover up the scriptures by then, and that's the main reason he wants to come."

"Okay, he can come next week; I'll tell him Sunday."

"There was something else I wanted to talk to you about." Izzy plucked up courage and repeated to Cathy all that Pastor Peter had said about receiving salvation through Jesus.

"Yes, I've heard him preach about that. In fact it had quite an effect on me at the time, but then – you know how it is. Maybe I'll think about it one day. There's plenty of time!"

"Exactly what I thought," agreed Izzy.

Pulling up outside the cottage, Cathy said, "I do so love this place, Izzy; I can't wait to move in!"

"I see they've taken the car away," Izzy said.

"Just as well; it was an upsetting reminder," Cathy replied. "Bring the milk and cake in, would you?"

Making their way upstairs and into the room, Cathy said, "The air in here smells musty! Can you open the window, Iz, and let some fresh air in?"

160

"Probably from being shut up all weekend; we should have left the door open," Izzy replied, wrinkling her nose.

"I didn't really get a chance to show you the scriptures last Friday, with all that was going on. What do you think then?" Cathy said. "Do we keep them or lose them?" she asked.

"I know they're an intriguing part of the history, but I must admit I don't think I'd keep them if this is going to be a nursery. What are you going to do - cover them back up again?" Izzy replied.

"The boarding looks nice, but it's odd there's only a yard or so of it. I wonder why they didn't cover the whole wall. It looks as if it's covering up something; maybe there's something behind it. What do you think?" Cathy said.

The entry in father Joel's book came to Izzy: '*On the 13th May: A heavy burden lies within my soul that the evil in the room is not at rest. But, by the grace of God, the door to the room has* **been boarded up**, *which is now the only containment of the evil spirit that lies within. God help anyone living in such a place if the boarding were to be removed, for who could stand such evil that would befall him?*'

A door to a room has been boarded up. Could this be the boarding that he was referring to? If so, then the boarding that Cathy was about to remove was containing the source of evil in the house!

"A lot of the nails are already sticking out; pass me that lever over there; I want to see if I can remove one of these boards."

"No, Cathy! If you do, Pastor Peter won't be able to see the scriptures."

"No problem. All I need do is take a photo of them," Cathy said taking her phone out. "There - all done; now where's that lever?"

Izzy, running out of excuses to stop her, could only hope that she was wrong about what was behind the boarding, and passed her the lever.

Slowly the first board gave way to the lever, then the second, beginning to reveal some dark oak board.

"Look, Izzy! There *is* something behind!"

In her excitement, Cathy set about levering off the rest of the boards. "It's a *door,* that's been boarded up! I wonder how long it's been covered?"

"Don't open it, Cathy!"

"What do mean: *'don't open it'*? Do you think I'm just going to stand here and look at a door that I've just discovered and not see what's in there?"

"I mean wait, let's just think before opening it; that's all I'm saying. It's probably not been opened for centuries; we don't know what's lurking behind it."

"Like what? What could possibly be in there that can harm us?" Cathy asked.

"Rats or something."

"Rats? Now you're being silly! I would have heard them or smelt them."

"It's covered in dust and dirt, Cathy; let me clean it off before you open it."

By now, Izzy felt sure this was the door Father Joel was referring to. Desperate to delay Cathy from opening it, she said, "If there *are* rats, there might be some kind of disease on the wood, and it wouldn't be good for you - in your condition. Why don't I bring some disinfectant with me tomorrow to wash the door?"

"Hello! What do you think these are, Izzy?" she said, holding up her gloved hands. "Give me the hoover – that'll do it."

As she started to vac the years of dust from the door, she stopped as she could see carved into the door some lettering. "What does that say?"

"I don't know; it's not very clear, is it?" replied Izzy, peering.

"I can make the first three words out: 'enter and be', but, correct me if I'm wrong, the last word is in Latin. 'δαμεδίουϛ'. Doesn't that mean 'damned'?"

Izzy read it out: "Enter and be damned'. Don't open it, Cathy! Please don't open it. Let's wait until Pastor Peter gets here."

"I've never seen you so concerned, Izzy. It's as if you know what's behind that door, and that would be impossible, wouldn't it?"

"Oh, Cathy, I didn't know what to do; I didn't want to spoil your dream. It's what Father Michael wanted to see me about. He had found the old priest's diary, saying that he had performed the exorcism of an evil spirit from behind that door and that's why it had been boarded up all these years."

"What? Are you saying the place is haunted?"

"A little more than haunted, Cathy; it's cursed."

"Cursed! Who cursed it?"

"A man called 'Tobias Spry' back in the 1500's."

"But why would this Tobias Spry curse the cottage?"

Not wanting to freak Cathy out by telling her *she* was cursed, Izzy said, "I don't know, Cathy. Father Michael couldn't find out, but he said that for it to have lasted all these years it must have been due to something bad that had happened to him. Apparently, the number '13' has got something to do with it; something dreadful always seems to happen on the 13th. Do you remember when we went to the church, we found out that the cottages where built in 1513, and Henry Derwin was hanged in 1513?"

"Yes."

"Well, after we left, he found out a lot more. Henry Derwin's son, Thomas, died here on the 13th, Margaret

163

(his daughter) died here on the 13th, and Father Joel performed the exorcism on the 13$^{th"}$.

"Couldn't it be a lot of coincidences?" Cathy asked.

"There's more Cathy. The old lady, Miriam Myrtle, moved in here in 1913, and lost her husband in the war the same year. I know he didn't die in the house, but it seems that, because she did, it must have affected him. Then she died, wait for it, on the 13th. And, lastly, Father Michael; do you realise what the date was when he died in this room?"

There was silence from Cathy, and then she said: "The 13th?"

"Yes. All too much of a coincidence - wouldn't you say?"

"Is that why all these scriptures about protection were written on the boarding?"

"I reckon so, Cathy. That's why I don't think you should go in there until Pastor Peter gets here."

"So, is he going to perform an exorcism, or doesn't he believe in all that?"

"He said that he thinks it will probably not be necessary, but he's happy to come here and see if he feels there's anything sinister in the place."

"But if bad things always happen on the 13th, then surely I'll be safe having a look in there now?"

"No, it's not worth taking a chance; we don't know for sure if anything has happened on any other dates," Izzy said firmly.

"Just a peek?"

"No!" Look, I must use the bathroom; promise me you won't go in there?"

"Yes, yes, I promise."

Cathy waited until Izzy was in the bathroom, then reached out to lift the latch of the door, but it didn't move. She knew she didn't have long before Izzy returned, so she picked up the lever and put it under the latch. It started to move. She was ready to open the door.

With a creaking sound from the old rusted hinges, the door opened. The stale air rushed towards her and filled her nostrils and throat, making her cough. What she was seeing hadn't been seen by anyone in centuries. It was a small, dark room. As she shone the torch around, the beam shone on the silver clasp of a scroll lying in the dust on the floor. She picked it up and unrolled it then, as she was trying to understand the words, she heard the scream.

"Cathy!"

Instantly the door slammed shut, with Cathy inside.

19

Opening the door, Cathy said, "Nice one, Izzy. You scared the life out of me!"

"I didn't do anything! When I saw you'd gone in there, I just panicked and called out your name."

"That was bad enough, but slamming the door like that scared me more."

"Cathy, I didn't touch the door; it slammed on it's own!"

"Oh come on, Izzy."

"Cathy, I swear to you; I didn't touch the door."

Cathy looked at the open window in the nursery and said, "It must have been the wind."

Izzy glanced outside. The tree leaves were completely still.

"Look what I found in there; it's a scroll with a lot of Latin written on it. This time I haven't a clue what it says; any ideas?" Cathy said handing it to her.

"No. Maybe we can ask Pastor Peter on Sunday, if he can read Latin, or I could go on the Internet and try to translate it?"

"That's fine; I'll leave it with you. I think that little room will make a good toy room, once I've given it a scrub and a couple of coats of paint."

"Cathy, haven't you taken any notice of what I've told you about what's in there?"

"To be honest, Izzy, no. I love history and old things, but I really don't believe in curses and all that stuff, and if you don't believe in it, it can't hurt you. Besides, I love that little room - it's cute, and I'm not going to let some stupid old curse nonsense stop me from living here."

"Well, maybe you'll listen to Pastor Peter when he comes."

"Don't hold your breath, Izzy! Stop worrying; nothing's going to happen!"

"Well, I think we made progress today! I don't know about you, Izzy, but I could do with a nice long soak in a hot bath, she said pulling up outside Izzy's house."

"Me too."

"Same time tomorrow?"

"Okay."

Cathy reached across to the open passenger window and called out, "Stop worrying!"

Hearing the key in the front door, Cathy poured out George's usual glass of wine.

"How was your day, Mum; finished the place yet?" George said, patting her on the tummy as he sat down beside her.

"What's this 'Mum' business?" Cathy asked.

"I thought it was appropriate, as you *are* going to be one."

"Ha, ha," she laughed. "Do you want the good news or the bad news?"

"Well, after the news you told me last Friday, you'd better give me the good news first!"

"The cottage has given up one more of its secrets. I've found another room!" she said excitedly.

"Another room?"

"Well, not really a room, more of a large cupboard. It will make a lovely toy room. It was hidden behind some boarding, and, by the amount of dust and dirt in there, I don't think it's been seen for centuries. Ask me what I found in there?"

"Okay, what did you find?"

"A scroll written in Latin! Izzy's taken it home to try and translate it."

"I can see why you were excited! Now what's the bad news?"

"The cottage has a curse on it, which is a load of old twaddle!"

"Whoa, whoa, slow down, what do you mean *a curse*?"

"According to Izzy, Father Michael, the one who died, did some research. He told her that a fellow called 'Tobias Spry' back in the 1500's put it there. Izzy's freaking out about it; I told her not to worry, but you know what she's like! She's been like a mother hen all day."

"Are you sure there's nothing to worry about? Obviously, I don't believe in stuff like that but, if a priest should go to the trouble to find out about it and tell Izzy, he obviously had reason to be concerned. So what is this curse supposed to do?"

"Apparently it kills people on the 13th of the month, according to Izzy. She says it's been happening since the cottage was built. I told her, it's a lot of coincidences and rubbish."

"What did she say to that then?"

"She has a list that she made with Father Michael at his church and tried to convince me with it. Can we stop talking about it, George; I've had Izzy going on about it all day! I just want to snuggle up here with you and enjoy my wine."

"Sure," he said, lifting his arm so that she could cuddle up him.

Izzy had spent the evening on the Net, translating the scroll. Because it was so late when she'd finished, she'd left it till the morning to tell Cathy what it said.

After tooting the horn, Cathy sat in the car waiting.

"Before you ask: yes, I've got the milk and cake, and I've translated the scroll," Izzy said.

"You've done it?" Cathy asked, surprised. "What does it say?'

"It's an exorcism prayer. The mystery is: why was it in there? I know, from the old priest's diary, he performed an exorcism in the room. I can only assume that he must have dropped it, but why he would leave it there, I can't fathom, especially with a silver clasp on it. It would have been worth a lot of money in those days. It makes you think he must have left the room in a hurry; wouldn't you agree?"

"Well, if he was old, maybe he was forgetful; or he thought it had to be left in there for it to work. Who knows? There could be a hundred reasons for it being there. Now, can I get going, or are we going to sit here all day talking about spooky stories?" Cathy said, driving off.

"I can tell you word for word what the translation says if you like."

"No! By the way, I've got some news. The police have contacted me. Apparently, there was some suspicion about Father Michael's death. They had a post mortem done and found that he choked to death from *smoke inhalation*! Then there was the discrepancy over time of death because we said he'd only been left for about fifteen minutes, which wasn't time for rigor mortis to set in. Fortunately for us, they talked to his housekeeper who assured them he was alive and well at breakfast a couple of hours before he arrived at the cottage."

"Oh my goodness, do you think they suspected us of foul play?"

"Well, I suppose they must have – when you think about it. None of it makes any sense. Anyway, they're not proceeding any further with it, thank goodness."

"Yes, we could have been in a difficult position – when you think how it must have looked. But *smoke inhalation*? Mind you, do you remember how his clothes smelt of smoke?"

They made their way into the nursery, to find that the door of the small room was shut.

"Izzy, did you close that door last night, after I told you I wanted it left open to air the room?"

"No, I left the room first; you were right behind me," Izzy replied.

A doubtful thought came to Cathy about the room, but she quickly dismissed it. "It must have swung too when we closed the main door."

Izzy could see, by the position of the latch, that it had to be lifted to shut the door, and that, swinging on its own, that wouldn't have been possible. As though to confirm her thoughts, when Cathy tried to lift the latch she couldn't move it until she asked Izzy to pass her the lever.

"If we wash all the walls and beams down this morning, we can paint it this afternoon. I'll start vacuuming, if you go and get some water," said Cathy, eager to get started.

Izzy was still anxious about leaving Cathy on her own, so she said, "I'll do the vacuuming; you go and get the water."

"Fine, whatever," Cathy replied.

Because Izzy felt uneasy as she entered the room, she propped the door open. The thick layers of dust were soon vacuumed up by the time Cathy had returned.

"You were quick!" Cathy said.

"I didn't want to be in here longer than necessary," Izzy replied.

"You don't still think there's something macabre in here, surely? There's nothing to worry about! Come on out and let me in there, so that I can wash the timbers down."

Izzy stepped out but stood by the door, watching Cathy work. As she made her way round the walls washing them, she stopped and stood back from the timbers.

"Look at that, Izzy! It looks like a face in the grain of that timber."

Izzy went back in and stood beside Cathy. "You're right; it is a face, and it has a nasty, sinister look. I don't like it, Cathy; it gives me the creeps!"

"Don't be silly! I quite like him; I'm going to call him 'Old Tobias'; he's part of the charm of the place. And look at this on the edge; there are some Roman numerals carved on the beam. Pass me a brush." Cathy brushed hard to remove the dirt and dust from the numbers. "X111. That's thirteen, isn't it?"

"Yes, I wish you'd take this curse business seriously, Cathy."

"I told you, if you don't believe in it, it can't hurt you," Cathy said resolutely, as she started to scrub the face. "There, Tobias, you've had a wash after all these years! You're quite handsome now," she said, standing back and admiring her work.

"Cathy, the water in the bucket! Look, it's red!"

Cathy looked down. "Where did that come from?"

"It wasn't that colour when you did the others. It's come out of the beam with the face on," Izzy said alarmed.

"There must be some red dye in the wood that's come out with the water."

"But, Cathy, it's not water in the bucket; I think it's blood!" Izzy said examining her finger as she removed it from the bucket.

"It's not blood; it's water, Izzy. Now, stop being dramatic!"

"Cathy, it's too thick for water. Please, let's get out of here!"

"It's the dirt and dust mixed with the red dye that makes it look like blood. You can go if you like; I'm going to finish this room."

Izzy could see she was determined to stay in the room, and decided not to go.

"Well, what do you think, Izzy? Doesn't that look good, now it's had a coat of paint?"

"Yes. Now can we go? I want to be home early tonight," she said, looking at her watch. She'd made up the excuse to get Cathy to leave.

"Izzy, give me a chance to clean up!"

"That's alright; we can do it tomorrow."

"Well, let me prop the door wide open so it dries in there."

Propping it with a broom, Cathy took one more admiring glance at her work, and said, "I'm pleased with that."

"Yes, yes, now can we go?" Izzy said from behind her, pushing her out of the room.

"Goodbye, Tobias; see you tomorrow," Cathy called out behind her. "Stop pushing me, Izzy!"

172

As hard as she tried to relax, Izzy couldn't stop worrying about Cathy. Despite it being so late, she knew if she was to get any sleep she had to make a call that would reassure her.

"Pastor Peter, it's Izzy Earnshaw here, Cathy Dawson's friend."

"Yes, Izzy, what can I do for you?"

"I'm sorry to ring you so late, but I just needed to speak to someone."

"That's alright, it's what I'm here for."

"I spoke to you last Sunday about Cathy; I was concerned about her living in her new cottage."

"Yes, I remember, you were going to arrange for me to visit the place. By the sound of your voice, I gather something's happened?"

"Well, yes. We found a hidden room and I know it's the source of the curse."

"What makes you think it's the source?"

"Because there's an evil looking face on one of the beams and the number thirteen carved into it, plus there's an awful sense of fear in there."

"Does Cathy feel it?"

"No, that's the problem; she doesn't. She thinks it's a load of hocus pocus, even though the door of the room mysteriously slammed shut on its own in front of her. I keep trying to tell her that things like this are real, but she won't believe it. She even gets cross with me when I talk about it, but something deep down inside tells me not to leave her on her own."

"Then don't, Izzy. Usually it's that gut feeling you should trust. As I said before, I will come, but I can't until Cathy invites me."

"Can you not sort of pretend to be interested in the cottage and say to her Sunday that I've been telling you all about the place and you'd love to see it?"

173

"Izzy, I'm a Pastor; I don't do 'pretends'. Anyway, I am genuinely interested in it."

"Sorry, Pastor; it's just that I'm so concerned."

"I know. Look, speak to her and say that I've been chatting with you and that I've asked if I could see the cottage."

"I've already told her that, but she said she wanted to have the place finished before she showed you. I'm worried that something bad might happen to her before then. I think she might just listen to you. Couldn't you come before Sunday if I get her to agree?"

"Sorry, Izzy, the problem is I'm on a tight schedule. The earliest I could get there is the 14th, although if things go to plan for me, I might be able to squeeze the day before."

Izzy thought for a moment, and said, "No, that's the 13th! That's when something bad usually happens."

"If that's the case, there's no better time for me to see what might go on."

"Please don't come on your own, Pastor; I would hate anything to happen to you as well."

"I won't be on my own, Izzy. I'll have several of my people with me, all committed Christians. Rest assured, if it's as bad as you've been telling me, we'll be prepared. We have God on our side and no evil force is a match for Him. Now, tell her I will speak to her Sunday, and meanwhile, I will pray for her safety and yours."

"Thank you, Pastor Peter. I feel a bit better now I've spoken to you."

"God bless, Izzy. See you Sunday."

"You're quiet this morning, Izzy. Did you have a bad night?"

"No, I just have a lot on my mind."

"Spill!"

174

"Don't be cross, but because I'm so concerned that you'll be living at the cottage, I phoned Pastor Peter."

"What did you do that for? I told you there's nothing to worry about!" Cathy said raising her voice.

"Cathy, what's got into you? You've never spoken to me like that before. As I said, it was because of your attitude that 'there's nothing to worry about'; you're worrying the life out of me."

"So what did he have to say?" she said in a quieter tone.

"He just said that he'd talk to you on Sunday."

"And what makes you so sure I'm going to church on Sunday?" she said, raising her voice again.

"Okay, I'm sorry. It's only because ....."

"You're worried about me," Cathy said, interrupting her. "I'm not sure I want you with me today if you're going to keep on about it."

Izzy now knew there was definitely something wrong with Cathy. Although they'd only recently started going to church, she was usually keen not to miss it; also her gentle nature was changing into an aggressive one. As the last thing she wanted was for Cathy to be on her own, she said, "I promise you won't hear another word from me on the subject."

"As long as I don't! There's a lot of work to be done; I want the upstairs finished by the weekend."

Cathy made her way into the nursery to check the paintwork in the new-found room, with Izzy close behind her. "I *know* we propped that door open last night! It's *impossible* for it to have shut – nobody's been here!"

Izzy didn't say a word; she just watched her lever up the catch of the door.

"How did all those red stains get there?" Cathy said running her hand over the wall panel. "It seems as if it's come from the beam; it's ruined the wall! If there's one thing I hate, it's going over old work!"

Izzy still didn't say anything. She could tell Cathy wasn't in a good mood from their earlier conversation, and the ruined paintwork had only made it worse.

"Why don't you let me repaint the wall panel and you can make a start in the other room?" Izzy said, trying to lighten the atmosphere.

"Okay, that would be good," Cathy, replied.

Before Izzy went into the room she made sure the door was firmly propped open. She wasn't going to take any chances of being shut in by whatever evil force was in there.   As she started to paint, she could feel an uneasiness building up within in her, which made her slap the paint on rapidly.

"Are you done yet?" she heard Cathy calling out from the other room; it gave her the reassurance of someone else being around, even though it was aggressive.

"Yes, just finishing!" She couldn't wait to get out of the oppressive atmosphere, and go to join Cathy. As she went towards the door of the nursery, she noticed a red handprint on the edge of the door; then as she stepped into the hall she could see another on the wall.

"Cathy," she said as she went into the other room, "Let me see your hands."

"What?"

"Show me your hands!"

As Cathy turned them over, they saw that the hand she had used to run over the stains was now deep red.

"I don't understand! The red on the wall was *dry* when I touch it!"

"You've left your handprint on the door in the nursery and on the hall wall. Wash it, Cathy, now! Get it off you!" Izzy urged in a panicky voice.

Cathy went to the bathroom and ran her hands under the tap. "There must be some strong sort of dye in that beam," she said as she soaped and scrubbed them. When she took her hands out of the water to inspect them, she cried out in alarm: "Izzy, it's not coming off!"

"How long do you think it'll be before it wears off?" Cathy said still staring at her hand.

"I don't know. Maybe you can wear gloves until it does," Izzy replied.

"Be serious! Do you think I'm going to go around wearing *gloves* for I don't know how long? And how am I going to explain this to George?" she said crossly.

"More to the point, Cathy, what's *your* explanation for it? And don't say: 'dye'!"

"Look, if you can't say anything useful, keep quiet. I don't know what it is, but there has to be a logical explanation, and I'm not letting something like this stop me getting on and finishing the place!"

Izzy knew about Cathy's determination to get the decorating done, but what she didn't know was what Tobias Spry had in store.

20

"**Y**ou're early!"

"You know me, Cathy; I don't like being late for church. Good Saturday night?"

"Quiet one, with a bottle of wine," Cathy replied.

"What did George say about your red hand?"

"That's the strangest thing! When I went to show him, there was no dye on it! It had completely disappeared. All I know is that it was there at the house. Can you imagine if I'd told him I had this red dye on my hand and it wouldn't come off? He would have thought I'd lost the plot and was overworking or something."

"I must confess I didn't notice whether it was there when we drove home Friday, but the good thing is: it's off."

"Amen to that, Izzy."

"Hark at you with your 'amen'! Are you getting yourself ready for church?" Izzy said laughing.

Cathy gave a little chuckle.

"Morning Izzy, Cathy. It's good to see that you made it this morning, Cathy."

With a quiet voice, Cathy replied: "Good morning, Pastor. I hear that you'd like to come and see my cottage?"

"Yes, I would love to, if that's okay? Izzy's been telling me about all the finds the cottage has been giving up, especially the boarded-up room."

Cathy darted a look at Izzy. Deliberately avoiding the subject of the room, she said, "I've only got the upstairs finished."

"That's fine. It will be good to see the 'before' and 'after' of the place. I must confess I love old buildings, especially those with some interesting history. I'm attending a conference not far from your place with some of the other pastors next Wednesday morning. If you didn't mind them coming as well, we could drop in during the afternoon. I'm sure they would love to see it too, but only if it's convenient?"

Sarcastically, she said to herself, *Whoopee do - a party!* "Yes that's fine."

"You sound a little hesitant, Cathy," Pastor Peter said.

"No, It's fine; I'll write the address down for you before we go."

"Could you email it; that way I won't forget," he replied.

"Okay."

"I could shoot you, Izzy!" she said, driving home. "I know what you're up to."

"It can't hurt, Cathy. Pastor Peter's visit will prove one of two things: either that you're right (and I'm worrying over nothing), or that there is something sinister there, in which case I was right to worry."

"Whatever!" Cathy replied with an exasperated sigh.

"You're in a bad mood today. I'll see you tomorrow; Bye Cathy."

"Yeah."

"Are we in a better mood this morning?" Izzy said, closing the car door.

"I don't know what you mean," Cathy replied.

Izzy changed the subject. I think we should make good progress this week, seeing the rooms downstairs are not too bad. What do you think - about two weeks?"

"I hope so, providing we don't keep having visitors."

Izzy kept quiet for the rest of the journey.

Cathy put the big old key into the lock. The door made its usual creaking noise as it opened, and they went in, eager to get started. The cottage still smelled musty in the downstairs rooms.

"You know what, I'm going to pick some flowers! That'll cheer up this room, and make it smell nice," Izzy announced.

When she came back in, she put the flowers in an old jar on the table and, as she was arranging them, the room seemed to change around her. She saw herself dressed differently, in what seemed to be simple period clothes. The crackling sound of a fire and the smell of tobacco smoke made her look up from the flowers; then, as she turned towards the fireplace, she saw a man sitting in front of the fire, smoking a pipe with his eyes closed. Opening his eyes, he looked straight at her and said, "Isabella."

"Izzy, what are you staring at? Are you having one of your funny moments again?" said Cathy, coming in from the other room.

"That was strange! The room changed there for a moment; one minute I was arranging the flowers, then it was as if I was inside someone else's body looking out. I seemed to be in the past. There was a man sitting in front of the fire. He spoke to me – called me 'Isabella'."

"No... you heard me calling you."

"Cathy I know what I heard; it was 'Isabella'. I even had a different dress on; I can see it now - long with flowers on it. I know you won't agree with me, Cathy, but I think I somehow saw a flashback in time, when Isabella was in this room."

"You're right, Izzy! I wouldn't agree with you; I think you're letting the history of this place run away with your imagination. Are you coming, or am I going to do all the work next door? By the way, those flowers look rubbish."

Izzy couldn't make out whether what Cathy had just said about the flowers was serious or not, but it had sounded as though she meant it. Izzy was concerned, as she had never heard her talk like that before. As she followed her next door she stopped and glanced back into the room; as she did, she caught a whiff of tobacco smoke.

"I think this room is slightly bigger than next door; it'll make a fine lounge - and I just love that big fireplace! Can you imagine: on a winter's evening, sitting here in front of a log fire. I'll bet there's been many a person, or family, doing just that over the centuries. I can't wait to move in, Izzy; I can't wait!"

Izzy started to feel somewhat perplexed at Cathy's changing moods. She wasn't the Cathy she knew. Her mind took her back to when she had first met her at the night school classes, where they were studying the history of buildings in the Tudor period. By the time the course had finished, they had formed a close friendship, and she knew her well enough to know that this was most unlike her. Suddenly a strange grin came on Cathy's face, giving Izzy a feeling of uneasiness. "Yes I can visualize it; it's a nice room. So what colour have you chosen?" she replied.

"I got a very pale mint green - to contrast with the oak beams, yes?"

181

"Yes, it will look good and also the colour seems to fit with the period," replied Izzy.

As the room was so big, it took them most of the day. They finished up and were admiring the room, when suddenly: BANG!

"What was *that*?" Cathy said.

"It sounded like it came from the room above us," Izzy replied.

The pair of them rushed upstairs, with Cathy leading. She made her way into the nursery. "What!" The door to the little room had shut again. "I know you left the door propped open Friday - I went in there to check your work after you'd finished."

"Oh, did you? And?" Izzy said.

"Yeah, good job. This catch is stuck again; this is so annoying! Out in the hall, Izzy, should be a big screwdriver; get it for me will you?"

Cathy prised the catch upwards and the door opened.

"That's impossible!" she said, staring at the wall Izzy had repainted. "It's come back!" she said, as she moved to rub her hand over the red stain.

"No, Cathy!"

It was too late. As she slowly turned her hand over, it was stained red.

"Not again!" Cathy said, looking at her hand in exasperation.

"I tried to stop you."

"Well, at least I know it does come off, and this time I'll get a chance to see when it does. Before we go, I'm going to tie the catch of the door to the window catch. I'm not saying there's anything spooky, Izzy, but it is a little weird the door keeps shutting."

"If you say so, Cathy. Can we go home now?"

They made their way downstairs into the kitchen area that led to the front door.

"How's your hand - is the red stain still there?" Izzy asked.

"Yep, still there," she replied, examining it.

"You don't seem to be freaking out about it so much; maybe you'll be able to tell George."

"We'll see," Cathy replied.

As she turned the key to lock the door, Cathy could see that the stain was disappearing.

"Are you seeing this, Izzy?"

"Yes, I'm seeing it. It seems that when you're out of the house, it goes."

"That's when it must have gone last time, and I didn't notice," Cathy said.

"So what do you think, Cathy?"

"About what?"

"The red stain disappearing."

"As I keep saying, there has to be a rational explanation for all this."

21

"Did someone knock at the door?" Cathy said, pausing with paintbrush in hand.

"I didn't hear anything," replied Izzy, turning the radio down.

"Hello! Cathy, it's Pastor Peter!"

"Oh no, not him!"

"Cathy, it's the pastor!"

She sighed and put down her brush. "I forgot he was coming." Opening the window, she said, "One minute - I'll be right with you." Turning back she said: "Izzy, is there any paint on my face? How is my lippy?" She pressed her lips together and ran her fingers through her hair, hoping it looked tidy.

Mildly surprised, Izzy looked at Cathy, recalling that she'd never been vane about her appearance before. Hastily, she said, "You're fine. Go and open the door!"

"Come on in, Pastor. You'll have to excuse the mess, and my appearance. I forgot you were coming."

"You know Pastor John, and Pastor Lyn?" he said, introducing them.

"I've seen you in church but we haven't really spoken yet," she said shaking their hands. You know Izzy?"

"Hello, Izzy," they all said.

"Well, this is my little cottage. Before I show you around, I must warn you there's wet paint in the other room."

"We'll be careful," Pastor Lyn said.

"I didn't realise it was so big inside."

"There are another two floors above, Pastor," replied Cathy. "Mind your head as we go up the stairs. These are the attic rooms, small - but apparently they used to sleep up here."

"They sure have character - these old places, but I'm not sure if I could live in one. I'm a modern day person, well at least my wife is," remarked Pastor John.

"Peter tells me that you've found a hidden room; can we see it?"

Cathy gave Izzy one of her accusing looks.

"Yes, Lyn, it's on the floor below," Izzy said, leading the way down the stairs with Cathy behind her.

Izzy and Cathy stood back while the others went into the room.

"See, this is what I knew would happen; you tell one person, then everybody knows," Cathy said, so quietly that the others didn't hear. "I know why she said that; why didn't she come right out with it and say we've come to see your haunted room? Those church people lie, just like all the rest."

"Look, Cathy, if you're sure there's nothing untoward in there, then you have nothing to worry about; but if there is, then it's good that they're here. Let them do what they have to do."

"Well, I'm not standing around listening to a lot of mumbo jumbo talk! If you need me, I'll be downstairs. By the way you know it's the 13th today; not that it bothers

185

me, but if anything does happen to them, it's nothing to do with me!"

Izzy, already aware it was the 13th, went in with a feeling of uneasiness to join the others. She was torn between praying that nothing would happen, and hoping it *would* so that, for Cathy's sake, it could all be put to rest.

"Is Cathy not joining us?" Pastor Peter asked.

"No, I'm afraid she doesn't believe that there's anything wrong with the place or that your visit will make any difference."

"Just as well, her unbelief would only hinder what we have to do," remarked Lyn.

"So is the room behind this door?"

"Yes, Pastor." Izzy noticed that the cord Cathy had used to tie the door open was broken and now it was shut.

Pastor Peter tried to lift the catch, but it wouldn't move.

"You have to pry it up with a screwdriver; we always have this problem. It's as if it doesn't want to be opened," Izzy said, passing him the screwdriver.

"We'll see about that!" Pastor Peter said, prising the latch upwards.

He could feel an unnatural force pushing down against the screwdriver so the door would stay closed.

"Stronger is He that is in me, than he that is in the world," came from his lips.

The catch lifted and the door creaked open slowly, revealing the narrow room.

"I suggest we pray the Lord's protection over us, before we go in," Pastor Peter said.

They formed a circle and held hands. Pastor Peter began to pray. *"Lord as we go into the enemy's camp, surround us with protection; set a wall of fire around us so that no evil can come against us. We will not be afraid, because we know You are with us. You are our Rock, our*

Protector, our Strong Tower. With You, we will have the victory over what is in here. Lord, You are our light and salvation, so whom shall we fear? Lord, You are the strength of our life, of whom shall we be afraid? In Jesus' name we thank You. Amen."

The room was filled with several 'Amens'.

"Before you go in, I'm going to wedge the door open. It has a habit of closing on its own when someone is in there," Izzy said. "One other thing, if there is a red stain on the wall, don't touch it."

"Red stain? You mean this?"

"Yes! Don't touch it; it seems to have a lot to do with it all."

"Like what? We need to know everything, Izzy," Pastor Peter said.

"All I know is that the priest who died here had a red stain on him when they found him; to be exact, it looked very much like a handprint. Also, when Cathy touched it she couldn't get it off, until she went outside; then it disappeared before our eyes. Whatever it is, it's not good," she said, staying outside the room.

"Pastor Peter, do you feel what I'm feeling? The temperature in here seems to be dropping?"

"Yes, I'm feeling it too, Lyn."

Suddenly, the door started to shake violently, slowly moving the wooden wedge beneath it along the floor as though trying to trap them all inside.

"No, you don't!" said John, putting his shoulder to the door, keeping it open.

"In Jesus' name, we cast you out, you foul demon! Be gone!" shouted Lyn.

"Keep praying," Pastor John, said as he battled with the force trying to close the door.

The room started to fill with acrid smoke and foul odour, which made them cough and their eyes water.

187

"Lord, your Word says that if we make You our refuge (and we do), then no harm will come near us, so we say in Jesus' name, this smoke will have no effect on us and we will have the victory," Pastor Peter said with authority. "We don't know what name you have, but there is a name higher than any name and, at that name, you will bow! In Jesus' name be gone!"

The heavy evil presence in the room started to subside; the door stopped shaking and the air became clear.

"I think whatever it was has gone for now," said Pastor Peter.

"Praise the Lord! We give you thanks for the victory here today, Lord," Lyn said.

"Well, Izzy, you were right to suspect there was an evil presence here."

"Thank you, Pastor Peter, thank you!" she said, hugging him.

"I wouldn't get too excited, I'm afraid. I'm still concerned for Cathy – and you."

"But, you said yourself, whatever it was has gone!" said Izzy, confused.

"*For now.* It had to go when we spoke the Word of God and took authority over it in Jesus' name; but we are believers and God has given us His authority and protection. Correct me if I'm wrong, but Cathy (and you too, Izzy) haven't yet committed your lives to Jesus and accepted Him as your Lord and Saviour."

"But we go to church!" Izzy protested.

"Izzy, that doesn't make you a Christian. You could go around telling people you're married to the Prime Minister, but he would say he doesn't even know you. You need to have a *relationship with Jesus,* which happens when you tell him you repent of your sins and invite him into your life. Going to church isn't enough. If you haven't made

188

that commitment to Him, it's just empty religion. Cathy (and you) won't have any protection until you're ready to do that and I strongly urge you both to stay away from this place."

"Oh, my goodness," said Izzy, dismayed.

"I'll have a word with Cathy before we go and make sure she understands the danger," said the Pastor, patting Izzy on the shoulder.

"No – leave it with me. She's not in a very receptive mood at the moment. After you've gone I'll sit her down and make sure she listens."

"Are you sure, Izzy? Only this is really important, and I'm more than happy to speak to her."

"I'm sure. To be honest, I think she'll take it better from me – she wasn't that pleased when you arrived."

"Well, we'd better get going if we're going to miss the traffic in the town," he said as they made their way down the stairs.

"Cathy!" Izzy said as she put her head around the front room door, they're off now."

"Oh 'bye..." Cathy called out, "I'm in the middle of painting a wall."

Pastor Peter stuck his head round the door, "That's okay, Cathy. God bless; we'll see you Sunday."

"Yeah okay," she replied, half-heartedly.

Izzy escorted them out to their car. "Thank you all once again," she said.

"That's what we're here for, Izzy; see you Sunday. God bless."

Izzy watched them drive away and was turning back to the open front door, when it violently slammed shut on her, locking her out.

"Cathy, I'm locked out! Can you open the door?" she shouted through the letterbox.

But there was no answer from Cathy. Remembering that she was in the front room, Izzy made her way to the window and peered in, but couldn't see her. "Cathy!" she shouted out, "Cathy!" She ran back to the door and pulled and banged on it, in a futile effort to open it, still desperately shouting Cathy's name. Her knuckles were soon raw and she realised it was hopeless to keep trying. Sobbing in frustration, she gave up and ran back to the window.

While everyone was outside, Cathy had ventured upstairs to the little room to see what they had done. No sooner had she set foot into the nursery, the door slammed shut, trapping her in the room. She tried with all her might to open it but it seemed as though some sort of force was keeping it closed. She ran over to the window, hoping they were still in the drive chatting but, to her dismay, she saw that they had gone. She could hear the distant sound of Izzy's voice calling her name from outside, but couldn't see her. She tried to open the window to call out, but found that the catch wouldn't move. A cold shiver went down her spine, which made her turn to look behind her. Standing there was the gruesome, charred figure of a man, surrounded by flames, grinning at her. Cathy instantly stepped back in total shock. The figure started moving towards her, causing wherever he stepped to catch fire. All Cathy could do was scream: "Izzy!"

Standing in front of her, with the stench of foul breath, the figure rasped, "I've been waiting a long time for you, Catherine Derwin; you escaped me once, but now I have you!"

Whatever this thing was, she knew there was no escape from it. As the room began to fill with smoke and flames, she edged over to the window, as far away from him and the flames as she could get. She could see Izzy looking up at her and shouting in anguish as she started banging frantically on the glass and screaming, *"Izzy! Help me! Help me!"*

Frozen to the spot, Izzy couldn't believe what she was seeing. The thatch on the roof, although fire retardant, was now engulfed in flames, as was the room where Cathy was. To see Cathy's petrified face at the window, while being helpless to save her, was torment in itself; but it was the grinning face of an old man behind Cathy that seared itself into her mind. The last sound she heard was that of Cathy screaming in agony and terror, as the whole building was engulfed in flames.

"Anyone in there love?" It was the voice of a man who had been driving by, and had seen the flames from the road.

Izzy didn't answer.

"Love, *is anyone in there*?"

"Cathy! Cathy!" was all that came from her mouth.

"Are you saying that there's someone called Cathy in there?"

He could see that she was in shock, and put his coat around her. "We need the fire brigade and ambulance urgently," he said into his mobile.

By the time the emergency services arrived, the cottage was a mass of rubble and flaming timbers.

"Charlie! Do you live here?" One of the firemen asked, recognising the stranger as an old colleague.

"No, I saw the fire from the road and tried to help, but unfortunately it was too late."

"Too late?"

"Yeah, apparently there was a person called 'Cathy' in there. Judging by the intensity of the fire, she didn't have a chance of being recued; it gutted the place in minutes. I've never seen a fire so fierce! I shouldn't think you would find much left of her; in that heat, I would say she'd have been incinerated to ash. Talk about the 13th being unlucky for some; it sure was for her."

"Who's the woman with the medics?" the fireman asked.

"I don't know; I tried talking to her, but all she kept muttering was the name 'Cathy'. Can I get going? I'm supposed to be in a meeting. You know how to get hold of me."

"You still on the same number?"

"Yeah."

"Drop in and see us sometime; I know the lads would like to see you again."

"Will do."

PART 111

22

"Is that Mr Earnshaw?"

"Yes."

"Pastor Peter here, from The Community Church."

There was a silence at the end of the phone.

"Izzy's Pastor."

"Sorry, I had to think for a moment," John Earnshaw said, apologetically.

"I was wondering how Izzy's getting on?" Pastor Peter asked.

"She took it hard, losing her best friend. I still don't know all the details about what happened at the cottage. She was waking up in the night screaming, so the doctor has prescribed sleeping pills; she's not very coherent."

"Well, tell her we are praying for her and hope to see her soon - and hopefully you too. Please let us know if we can help in any way or you'd like a visit. It's been nice speaking to you, Mr Earnshaw, although I wish it had been under better circumstances."

"Thank you for phoning; I'll tell Izzy you called."

"How are you, Izzy? We've been praying for you; it's good to see you back in church."

"Thank you, Pastor Peter, I'm slowly getting there."

"We all handle grief in different ways; there's no time limit on it. If you want to stay behind after the service to talk, it's the least I can do for you. I'd like to think that you know I'm here for you anytime, Izzy."

"Yes, I know that Pastor. I would like that very much. As it happens there are some questions that have been bothering me."

"Sure, we'll have a coffee and talk in my office."

"Fire away, Izzy."

Izzy sat there looking for words. He could see by her silence and the look on her face that she was agitated.

"Speak out what's on your mind, Izzy; it's okay. Pent up feelings are better out than in."

"I see her face every night in my sleep, screaming my name. I don't understand why my friend had to die in such a terrible way. I thought God was more powerful than the devil. If he is such a loving, powerful God, why did he allow it to happen? So that's my question. Why, why?" she said, with tears running down her cheeks.

Pastor Peter reached across the table and held both her hands to comfort her. "Izzy, it's okay. We say all sorts of things when we're angry; God understands. That's probably the most asked question from people who've lost loved ones.

God is a God of love, but He is also a God of justice and He won't overrule man's original decision to hand authority over to the devil. (Do you remember the conversation we had about that before?) When terrible things happen, they are always the result of Satan's activity, yet most people blame God. That must be so hurtful for Him.

196

This isn't a perfect analogy but it might help to understand. Imagine this scenario:

A woman had a husband who was loving, kind, rich and powerful, and she had everything she could ever need or want. However, she was attracted by another man, who tricked her into thinking she could have *more* and *better* things, so she divorced her husband and married the second man. She soon found, though, that her life with the new husband was often marred by pain and tragedy, as were the lives of her children and their descendants. So whom did they all blame for the things that went wrong in their lives? The first husband!

Can you see how unfair that is? Just because the first husband was loving and powerful, it doesn't mean he could (or would) interfere in the woman's new marriage or the lives of her children."

Izzy sighed and said: "So basically, it's all a consequence of what Adam and Eve did. I remember you told me about that before. The other thing that worries me is what you said about accepting Jesus – that surrendering our lives to Him is the only way to Heaven. I did tell Cathy exactly what you told me, but she just said something about there's plenty of time to think about it. But, Pastor, she *didn't* have time! Well, not much."

"No, you're right. We all think we have plenty of time, but none of us knows when our last day will come, which is why we shouldn't put off the decision. What about *you*, Izzy? Are you ready to commit your life to Jesus and receive salvation?"

"I don't know, Pastor. After what's happened to Cathy, I can't even make small decisions; I need to think about it more. Is that alright?"

"Of course it is, Izzy. It's completely your decision –
but I wouldn't leave it too long, *especially* after what
happened to Cathy. Always, remember we're here to
help in any way we can."

23

"Billy, will you hurry up! You know Grandma gets upset if we're late."

Billy came rushing downstairs, to see his mum standing at the open door.

"Right, get in, and don't forget your seatbelt."

"Mum, why doesn't Grandma Izzy live in her house anymore?"

"She very old and, because her memory isn't very good, she's gone to live in a place where people can look after her."

"I miss staying with Gran."

"I know you do, Billy, but we see her every month."

"Suppose so."

"Good morning, Mrs Hawkins; morning, Billy," said the cheerful receptionist. "The doctor asked if you could have five minutes with him before you see your mother. If you take a seat, I'll let him know you're here. You can leave Billy here with me if you like; I'll keep an eye on him."

"Good morning, Mrs Hawkins; please take a seat," said the doctor, standing. "I wanted to have a chat with you about your mother. The dementia has got somewhat worse since your last visit. We know people with dementia sometimes relive a time in their past, but I've never come across a case like this."

"What do you mean?" she asked.

"Your mother seems to have taken on another identity, of someone living in Medieval, or maybe Tudor, times."

"What makes you say that?"

"By the way she talks, using words like 'ye', 'thee', 'verily' and such. Do you know who 'Tobias Spry' is? Or 'Catherine'? The reason I ask is that she seems to be having many conversations with the latter?"

"I wonder if she means Cathy, although she never called her 'Catherine'. Cathy was her best friend, who unfortunately died in a house fire some years ago; but I've never heard of a 'Tobias Spry', whoever he is."

"Mrs Hawkins, trauma can affect people in different ways; sometimes they get over it with time and others never get over it. For some, it can tip them over the edge. Now you've told me that, I feel the latter has possibly happened to your mother. Maybe she *is* confusing 'Cathy' with 'Catherine', but it doesn't explain the idiosyncrasy of her speech. Nevertheless, wherever she is, she seems to be happy."

"Will it be okay to see her, Doctor?"

"Of course. By the way, she's not answering to the name of 'Izzy' anymore; for some reason, she insists her name is '*Isabella*'."

"So, Sam, what do you think of my latest purchase? Do you think you can rebuild this pile of rubble?"

"I wouldn't be here now if I didn't think I could! Surely that's why you employed a specialist in building period properties."

"If you can salvage anything original, that would be good."

200

"By the look of that lot, Mr Jackson, I doubt if anything is salvageable. How many years has it been like this?"

"I haven't a clue! All I know is what they told me at the auction after I bought it on spec. Apparently, the property burned to the ground and the previous owner, before he died, left strict instructions in his will that it was not to be rebuilt. I suppose, as time went on, someone in the family got the restriction removed and decided to sell. By the state of the overgrowth, how long would you say it's been?"

"At least forty odd years, maybe more. We'll start clearing tomorrow, Mr Jackson."

"Good. I want this one turned around and on the market as soon as possible. I've got an American guy very interested in it; you know how they love these old properties. I'll drop by in a few days, to see how you're getting on."

"No problem, Mr Jackson."

"How's it going, Sam?"

"Fine, Mr Jackson, we've had a great find for you! I didn't think there could be *anything* salvageable amongst all that rubble, but we've uncovered a beam that would be perfect over the fireplace. That's as long as your buyer's not superstitious! It's got the number thirteen carved on it in Roman numerals. Come and have a look."

"If I'm not mistaken, it looks as though there's a grinning face in the grain. Oh, that's great - he's going to love it!"

"You've sold it already then, Mr Jackson?"

"Yes, to the American I told you about - a 'Mr Derwin'.